Help! **She was still tingling and zapping from having him take off her coat.**

This was such a dangerous moment. She only had to give the slightest hint of acceptance and Zac Corrigan would be kissing her. And she couldn't pretend that she didn't want to be kissed. His lips were so close, so scrumptious, so wonderfully tempting.

The air between them was crackling and sizzling. At any moment he was going to lean in…

Now she was struggling to remember why this was wrong. 'Zac, we can't—'

'Shh.' He touched her arm, sending dizzying warmth washing over her skin. 'Forget about the office for one night.'

'How can I? How can *you*?'

'Chloe, you're an incredibly sexy woman, and I'm absolutely smitten by you.'

Dear Reader

When I first started this story I planned to set it in my country—Australia. But when my editor asked for a Christmas theme I found myself wanting to write a 'fantasy' Christmas. As an Australian, I'm used to Christmases that are hot and often spent at the beach—and, while these Christmases are always wonderful, I found this time that my imagination had developed a hankering for a traditional cold climate festive season. I wanted my characters to wear coats and scarves, and to eat hot dinners and see beautiful snow.

So my fantasy took my characters to London, a city I love (as some of you might have guessed from other books I've written). When I added a drop-dead handsome and rich boss to the story mix, a super-conscientious PA, plus a newborn baby, I had all the ingredients for my favourite kind of Christmas.

I had so much fun writing Chloe and Zac's story. Thank you for picking up the book, and I hope you enjoy it. I would love to hear from you if you do.

Warmest wishes

Barbara

A VERY SPECIAL HOLIDAY GIFT

BY
BARBARA HANNAY

Published in Great Britain 2014
by Mills & Boon, an imprint of Harlequin (UK) Limited,
Eton House, 18-24 Paradise Road, Richmond, Surrey, TW9 1SR

© 2014 Barbara Hannay

ISBN: 978-0-263-24336-9

Reading and writing have always been a big part of **Barbara Hannay**'s life. She wrote her first short story at the age of eight for the Brownies' writer's badge. It was about a girl who was devastated when her family had to move from the city to the Australian Outback.

Since then, a love of both city and country lifestyles has been a continuing theme in Barbara's books and in her life. Although she has mostly lived in cities, now that her family has grown up and she's a full-time writer she's enjoying a country lifestyle.

Barbara and her husband live on a misty hillside in Far North Queensland's Atherton Tableland. When she's not lost in the world of her stories she's enjoying farmers' markets, gardening clubs and writing groups, or preparing for visits from family and friends.

Barbara records her country life in her blog, *Barbwired*, and her website is: www.barbarahannay.com

Recent books by Barbara Hannay:

SECOND CHANCE WITH HER SOLDIER
MIRACLE IN BELLAROO CREEK*
THE CATTLEMAN'S SPECIAL DELIVERY
FALLING FOR MR MYSTERIOUS
RUNAWAY BRIDE**
BRIDESMAID SAYS, 'I DO!'**

Bellaroo Creek!
**Changing Grooms*

This and other titles by Barbara Hannay are available in eBook format from www.millsandboon.co.uk

CHAPTER ONE

THE PHONE CALL that changed Chloe Meadows's life came when she was poised on tiptoe, on a chair that she had placed on top of a desk in a valiant attempt to tape a loop of Christmas lights to the office ceiling.

It was late on a Wednesday evening, edging towards nine p.m., and the sudden shrill bell in the silent, empty office was so unexpected Chloe almost fell from her precarious perch. Even so, she slipped as she scrambled down awkwardly in her straight grey business skirt and stocking feet.

She was slightly out of breath as she finally grabbed the phone just as it was due to ring out.

'Hello? ZedCee Management Consultants.' She wondered who would call the office at this late hour. On a Wednesday night.

There was a longish beat before she heard a man's distinctly English voice. 'Hello? I'm calling from London. Could I please speak to Mr Zachary Corrigan?' The voice was officious, like the command of a bossy teacher.

'I'm sorry. Mr Corrigan isn't in the office.' Chloe politely bit back the urge to remind the caller that it was well after office hours in Australia and that her employer was almost certainly at a social function.

On any given week night, Zac Corrigan was likely to be socialising, but that possibility had become a certainty *this* week, the week before Christmas, when almost everyone was at some kind of party. Everyone, that was, except Chloe, whose social calendar was *quiet* even at this busy time of the year.

Sadly, the red letter date in Chloe's festive season was the office Christmas party. This was the third year in a row that she'd put up her hand to be the party's organiser. She'd ordered the champagne, the wines and beer, as well as a selection of delicious canapés and finger food from François's. And she'd been happy to stay back late this evening to decorate the office with festive strings of lights, shiny balloons and bright garlands of tinsel and holly.

Secretly, she loved this task. When she'd first landed her job at ZedCee she'd also moved back home to care for her elderly parents, who weren't overly fond of 'gaudy' decorations, so this was her chance to have a little Christmas fun.

'To whom am I speaking?' the fellow from London barked into the phone.

'I'm Mr Corrigan's PA.' Chloe was used to dealing with bossy types, matching their overbearing manner with her own quiet calm. 'My name's Chloe Meadows.'

'Ms Meadows, this is Sergeant Davies from The Metropolitan Police and I'm ringing from The Royal London Hospital. I'm afraid the matter is urgent. I need to speak to Mr Corrigan.'

'Of course.' Instantly alarmed, Chloe forgave the policeman his bossiness and reached for a pen and paper.

She was appalled to think that this urgent matter was in any way connected to her boss. 'I'll call Mr Corrigan immediately and tell him to ring you.'

Sergeant Davies dictated his number, Chloe thanked him and her stomach clenched nervously as she connected straight to Zac Corrigan's mobile.

The zip in the young woman's black silk dress slid smoothly downwards and the fabric parted to reveal her delightfully pale back. Zac Corrigan smiled. She was lovely. Tipsy after too many champagne cocktails and without very much to eat, but at least they'd escaped the party early, and she was quite irresistibly lovely.

With a practised touch, he caressed the creamy curve of her shoulder and she giggled. Damn. Why did champagne make girls giggle?

Still. Her skin was soft and warm and her figure was exquisite and, for a repeat of the night they'd shared last weekend, Zac could forgive her giggling.

With a firm hand cradling her bared shoulders, he leaned closer to press a kiss to the back of her neck. His lips brushed her skin. She giggled again, but she smelled delicious and Zac's anticipation was acute as he trailed a seductive line of kisses over her shoulder.

The sweet moment was spoiled by the sudden buzz of his mobile phone and Zac swore beneath his breath as he sent a frustrated glare in the direction of the armchair where he'd dumped the phone along with his jacket and tie.

'I'll get it!' the girl squealed.

'No, don't bother. Leave it.'

Too late. She'd already wriggled free and was diving for the chair, laughing excitedly, as if answering his phone was the greatest game.

Chloe suppressed a groan when she heard the slightly slurred female's voice on the line.

'Hi, there!' a girl chirped. 'Kung Fu's Chinese Take-away. How can I help you?'

'Hi, Jasmine.' Chloe was unfortunately familiar with most of her boss's female 'friends'. They were usually blessed with beauty rather than brains, which meant they were always ringing him at work, and Chloe spent far too much time holding them at bay, taking their mes-sages, placating them with promises that Mr Corrigan would return their calls as soon as he was free, and gen-erally acting as a go-between. 'Hold the jokes,' she said now. 'And just put Zac on.'

'Jasmine?' The voice on the end of the line was slightly sloshed and distinctly peeved. 'Who's Jasmine?' Her voice rose several decibels. 'Zac, who's Jasmine?'

Oops. Under other circumstances, Chloe might have apologised or tried to reassure the silly girl, but tonight she simply spoke loudly and very clearly. 'This is Mr Corrigan's PA and the matter is urgent. I need to speak to him straight away.'

'All right, all right.' The girl was sulky now. 'Keep your hair on.' There was a shuffling, possibly stumbling sound. 'Mr Corr-i-gan,' she said next, sounding out the syllables in a mocking sing-song. 'Your PA wants you and she says you'd better hurry up.' This was followed by a burst of ridiculous giggling.

'Give that here!' Zac sounded impatient and a mo-ment later he was on the line. 'Chloe, what's up? What the hell's the matter?'

'An urgent phone call has come through for you from London,' she said. 'From the police. At a hospital.'

'In *London*?' There was no missing the shock in his voice.

'Yes. I'm afraid it's urgent, Zac. The policeman wants you to call him immediately.'

There was a shuddering gasp, then another sound that might have been—

No. It couldn't have been a sob. Chloe knew her ears were deceiving her. During three years in this job she'd never detected a single crack in Zac Corrigan's habitual toughness.

'Right.' His voice was still *different*, almost broken and very un-Zac-like. 'Can you give me the number?'

Chloe told him and listened as he repeated it. He still sounded shaken and she felt a bit sick. Normally, she refused to allow herself any sympathy for her boss's personal life, which was as messy as a dog's breakfast, as far as she was concerned. But this situation was different. Frightening. She couldn't recall any connection between her boss and London and she thought she knew almost everything about him.

'I'll let you know if I need you,' he said.

Zac was as tense as a man facing a firing squad as he dialled the London number. This emergency *had* to involve Liv. He was sure of it. He'd been trying to convince himself that his little sister was an adult now and quite capable of running her own life, especially after she'd ignored his protests and left for England with her no-hoper boyfriend... But...

Liv.

His baby sister...

All that was left of his family…

His responsibility…

'Hello,' said a businesslike English voice. 'Sergeant Davies speaking.'

'This is Zac Corrigan.' His voice cracked and he swallowed. 'I believe you're trying to contact me.'

'Ah, yes, Mr Corrigan.' The policeman's tone was instantly gentler, a fact that did nothing to allay Zac's fears. 'Can I please confirm that you are Zachary James Corrigan?'

'Yes.' What had Liv done? Not another drug overdose, surely? When he'd rung her two weeks ago, she'd promised him she was still off the drugs, *all* drugs. She'd been clean for over a year.

'And you're the brother of Olivia Rose Corrigan?'

'Yes, I am. I was told you're calling from a hospital. What's this about?'

'I'm sorry, Mr Corrigan,' the policeman said. 'Your sister died a short while ago as the result of a road accident.'

Oh, God.

It wasn't possible.

Shock exploded through Zac, flashing agonising heat, threatening to topple him. Liv couldn't be dead. It simply was *not* possible.

'I'm sorry,' Sergeant Davies said again.

'I—I see,' Zac managed. A stupid thing to say, but his mind was numb. With terror. With pain.

'Do you have any relatives living in the UK?' the policeman asked.

'No.' Sweat was pouring off Zac now. Vaguely, he was aware of the girl, Daisy, with the black dress dangling off her shoulders. She was hovering close, frowning at him, her heavily made-up eyes brimming with vacuous curiosity. He turned his back on her.

'Then I take it you'll be prepared to be our contact for any arrangements?'

'Yes,' Zac said stiffly. 'But tell me what happened.'

'I'll pass you onto someone from the hospital, sir. The doctor will be able to answer all your questions.'

Dizzy and sick, Zac waited desperately as the phone went through several clicks and then a female voice spoke.

'Mr Corrigan?'

'Yes,' he said dully.

'This is Dr Jameson from the maternity ward.'

Maternity? She was joking, surely?

'I'm very sorry, Mr Corrigan. Your sister was brought to our hospital after a vehicle accident. There were extensive head and chest injuries.'

Zac winced. Head and chest. The worst.

'Olivia was rushed to theatre and we did our very best, but the injuries were too extensive.' A slight pause. 'I'm afraid we couldn't save her.'

Zac went cold all over. So there it was. Two people had confirmed the impossible. His greatest fear was a reality. After all these years when he'd tried and failed with Liv, he'd now failed her abysmally...

And it was too late to try again.

He couldn't breathe, couldn't think. Horror lashed at him as he fought off images of Liv's accident. Instead he clung to a memory of his beautiful, rebellious young sister from years ago when she was no more than sixteen... He saw her on the beach, during a holiday on Stradbroke Island, her slim tanned arms outstretched, her dark gypsy hair flying in the sea wind, her teeth flashing white as she laughed and twirled with child-like joy.

He remembered it all so clearly. With her brightly co-loured sarong over a skimpy yellow bikini, she'd looked so tanned and beautiful. Innocent, too—or so Zac had thought—and, always, *always*, so full of fun.

That was how he'd thought of Liv back then—full of fun and life.

Now…he couldn't believe that her life had been extinguished.

'But we were able to save the baby,' the English doctor said.

Baby? Now Zac sank in weak-kneed horror onto the edge of the bed. What baby? How could there be a baby?

'Are you there, Mr Corrigan?'

He swallowed. 'Yes.'

'You're listed as your sister's next of kin, so I'm assuming you knew that Olivia was pregnant?'

'Yes,' he lied when in truth he'd had no idea. When he'd phoned Liv only two weeks ago, she hadn't said a thing about being pregnant. Right now, he felt as if the world had gone quite mad.

'Your sister was already in labour,' the woman said. 'We believe she was on her way to hospital when the accident occurred.'

'Right.' Zac sagged forward, elbows on knees. 'So—' he began and then he had to stop and take a shuddering breath, which wasn't much help. He forced himself to try again. 'So—this baby. Is it OK?'

'Yes, a beautiful baby girl, perfectly unharmed and born by Caesarean section only a couple of weeks before her due date.'

Zac pressed a shaking hand to his throbbing forehead. His stomach churned. He was sweating again. This woman was trying to tell him that some crazy twist of fate had snatched his beautiful sister's life and left a baby in her place. How bizarre was that?

He wanted to drop the phone, to be finished with this absurd conversation. No way did he want to deal with the gut-wrenching news that had just been so calmly delivered.

But, of course, he knew he had no choice.

With a supreme effort, he shut off the hurt and pain and, like the cool-headed businessman he usually was, he forced his mind to confront practicalities.

'I presume you've contacted the baby's father?' he said tightly, recalling the man who'd convinced Liv to run away with him. A guy from a band—a band no one had heard of—an older man with dreadlocks streaked with grey and restless eyes that could never quite meet Zac's gaze.

'Your sister wasn't able to tell us the name of the baby's father. There was a man in the car with her, but he assured us he was only a neighbour and not the father, and our blood tests have confirmed this.'

'But he could tell you—'

'I'm afraid he doesn't know anything about the father's identity.'

'Right.' Zac drew a deep, shuddering breath and squared his jaw. 'So this baby is, for all intents and purposes, my responsibility?' Even as he said this, he knew it hadn't come out right. He'd sounded uncaring and hard. But it was too late to try to retract his words. He could only press on. 'I'll...er...make arrangements to come over to London straight away.'

* * *

Chloe had just finished pinning the last decoration in place when her boss rang back.

'Chloe, I know it's late, but I need you to book me a flight to London.' His voice was crisp and business-like, but tight, too, the way people spoke when they were fighting to keep their emotions in check. 'You'd better make it the soonest flight possible. First thing tomorrow morning, if you can.'

'Of course, and would you like a hotel reservation as well?' Chloe hoped she didn't sound too surprised, or worried... If there was a crisis, the last thing Zac needed was an anxious, fussing PA.

'Yes, book a hotel room, please. Somewhere central.'

'No problem.' Already she was firing up her computer.

'And I'll need you to sort out those accounts with Garlands.'

Chloe smiled to herself. 'All done.'

'Already?' He sounded surprised. 'That's great. Well done.'

'Anything else?'

'Could you ring Foster's and tell them that Jim Keogh will represent me at tomorrow's meeting.'

'No problem.' Chloe paused, in case there were any more instructions. 'That's all then?'

'Actually, Chloe...'

'Yes?'

'You'd better book two flights to London. Just two one-way seats at this stage. I'm not sure how long I'll need to be over there.'

Ridiculously, Chloe's heart sank. An annoying reaction. Why should she care if her boss wanted to take the giggling girl who'd answered the phone with him on an all-expenses-paid trip to London? Of course, she couldn't help wondering how much use the girl be would if Zac had been called away to something urgent.

'What name for the second ticket?' she asked smoothly as the company's preferred airline's website came up on her computer screen.

'Ah...good question. Actually...'

Another pause. Chloe began to fill the boxes on the flights search. Point of departure... *Brisbane, Australia.* Destination... *London, UK.* Date of flight...

'How busy are you, Chloe?'

'Excuse me?'

'Could you spare a few days?'

'To fly to London?'

'Yes. This is an emergency. I need someone...capable.'

Chloe was so surprised she almost dropped the phone. Was Zac really asking her to go to—to London? *At Christmas?*

'I know it's short notice and it's almost Christmas and everything.'

Her head spun, first with shock and a fizz of excitement, and then with dismay as she thought about her elderly parents at home, waiting for her, depending on her to look after the shopping and to cook Christmas dinner and to drive them to church. They would never cope without her.

'I'm sorry, Zac. I don't really think I could get away at such short notice.'

As she said this, there was the sound of a door opening behind her and she jumped. Turning, she saw her boss striding into the office. Of course, he'd had his phone in the hands-free cradle while he was driving.

As always, Chloe's heart gave a pitiful little skip when she saw him, but at least she was used to that nuisance reaction now. She knew it wasn't significant—pretty much the automatic reaction shared by most women who encountered Zac Corrigan's special brand of tall, dark and handsome.

This evening he looked paler than usual and his grey eyes betrayed a shock he hadn't been able to shake off.

'If you can come with me, I'll pay you a hefty Christmas bonus,' he said as he strode across the office to Chloe's desk.

But he'd already paid her a generous Christmas bonus. 'Can you explain what this is about?' she asked. 'What's happened?'

What's happened?

Zac lifted his hand and rubbed at his brow, where a headache had been hovering ever since he took the call from the hospital and now throbbed with renewed and vicious vengeance.

'Are you all right, Zac? You look…'

Abruptly, Chloe pulled a swivel chair from the nearest desk and pushed it towards him. 'Here, sit down.'

He held up a hand. 'It's OK, thanks. I'm fine.'

'I'm sorry, but I don't think you are.'

To Zac's surprise, his PA took a firm grasp of his elbow, gripping him through his coat sleeve. 'I think you should sit down now before you fall down.'

Zac sat.

'Can I get you a cup of tea?'

If he wasn't feeling so strung out, he might have

smiled at this old-fashioned response from his conservative and over-conscientious PA. She was dressed in one
of her customary businesslike suits. Her white blouse
was neatly buttoned and tucked in, and there wasn't a
strand of her light brown hair out of place. Good old,
reliable Chloe.

He was so relieved to see her tonight. He'd been
desperate to get away from the giggling Daisy and, by
contrast, cool, collected Chloe was a reassuring and
comforting sight.

'I don't need tea,' he said. 'I'd just like to get these
flights sorted, and I could really do with your assistance in London.'

'I assume this is all because of the phone call…from
the hospital.'

'Yes.' Zac swallowed, trying to clear the sharp, per-
sistent pain that seemed to have lodged in his throat. 'I'm
afraid it wasn't good news,' he said with quiet resignation. 'It was bad. Really bad. The worst.'

'Oh, no… I'm so sorry.'

Sorry… Zac was sorrier than he'd ever thought possible. He looked away from the sympathy in Chloe's soft
brown eyes. Then, staring bleakly at a spot on the grey
office carpet, he told her the rest of his news…

When he finished, Chloe took ages to respond. 'I…I
don't know what to say,' she said at last. 'That's so terrible. I…I never realised you had a sister.'

'Yeah…well…' He couldn't bring himself to admit his
estrangement from Liv, or that he hadn't known about
the baby, that Liv had never even told him she was pregnant, that she almost hadn't told him about going to England.

How could he admit to this prim and conscientious

cliché of a secretary that his reckless sister's pregnancy was just another of the many secrets she'd hidden from him?

'I guess you'll need help...with the baby girl...if they can't find her father,' Chloe suggested awkwardly.

'Yes. I'll be it's...I mean...*her* guardian.' He knew this, because the one thing he'd insisted on after Liv's overdose was that she made a will. He'd hoped that a measure of reality would shake some sense into her. 'I couldn't possibly manage on my own.'

Babies had never registered on Zac's radar. He'd always supposed they were a dim possibility in his far distant future...when he eventually settled down and chose a wife and all that went with a wife... But, even though he was a godfather twice over, he'd never actually held a baby. There had always been plenty of women with willing arms and he'd been more than happy to buy expensive gifts and the best champagne to wet the baby's head and then stay well in the background...

'I'm sure we can find someone.' Chloe was busy at her computer screen, scrolling through some kind of spreadsheet.

'Find someone?' Zac asked, frowning. 'How do you mean? What kind of someone?' He didn't need to *find* someone. He had Chloe.

She turned back to him with a smile that was almost sympathetic. 'This is a list of your personal female contacts.'

'You have them on a spreadsheet?'

'Well, yes. How else do you think I manage to—?'

'All right, all right.' He gave an impatient wave of his hand. He knew Chloe was a marvel at managing his female friends—sending them the appropriate invitations or flowers, birthday or Christmas presents, get well cards, even, at times, offering excuses on his behalf…but he'd never given any thought to how she kept track of them.

'What about Marissa Johnson?' Chloe said now. 'She always struck me as sensible.'

'No,' Zac said curtly, remembering the awkward way he and Marissa Johnson had broken up. He jumped to his feet, seized by a fit of restless impatience. 'Look, there's no point in looking at that list. I don't want any of *them*. I want you, Chloe. We've worked together for three years now and I know you'd be perfect.'

To his surprise her cheeks went a deep shade of pink—a becoming shade of pink that unsettled him.

'I don't know very much about babies,' she said.

'Really?' Zac frowned at her. She was female, after all. 'But you know enough, don't you? You know how to put on a nappy. And when it comes to bottles and that sort of thing, you can follow instructions. It's just for a few days, Chloe. There's a remote possibility that I might have to bring this child home. I'll need help, just till I have everything sorted.'

Not that he had any idea how this problem could be sorted. At the moment he was still too shocked. Too sad. He didn't want to think about a little new life when Liv was—

'I'm sorry,' Chloe said quickly. 'I'd like to help, but I'm not really free to rush overseas at the drop of a hat. Not at this time of year. I have my parents to consider…'

'Your parents?' Zac frowned again. Why would a woman approaching thirty be so concerned about her parents? Then again, he knew he was out of touch with the whole family thing. His own parents had died when he was eighteen and he'd been managing without them for almost seventeen years.

But now there was a baby…a niece…another little girl who was his responsibility. A slug of pain caught him mid-chest. History was repeating itself in the most macabre way.

'It's Christmas,' Chloe said next, as if that explained everything. She looked up at the surprisingly attractive decorations she'd arranged about the office. 'Would you like me to look into hiring a nanny?'

Zac let out a weary sigh. 'The last thing I need now is to start interviewing nannies.'

'I don't mind doing the interviews.'

'No,' he snapped. 'We don't have time.'

Besides, for this delicate operation, he needed someone he already knew, a woman who was loyal and trustworthy, and sensible and efficient—and a woman who wouldn't distract him with sex.

Chloe Meadows ticked every box.

CHAPTER TWO

CHLOE COULDN'T QUITE believe it was actually happening. Here she was in the executive lounge of Brisbane International Airport, enjoying coffee and croissants with her boss, with a boarding pass for a flight to London in her handbag, a grey winter jacket and rosy pink scarf folded on the seat beside her, and a neatly packed carry-on bag at her feet.

She still wasn't quite sure how Zac had convinced her to do this, but from the moment he'd learned she had an up-to-date passport the pressure had begun. He'd argued that the company was winding down for the Christmas break anyway and, thanks to her superb organisational skills, the office Christmas party could run brilliantly without her.

He'd brushed aside her concerns that she knew very little about babies. After all, the child's father might yet be found.

To Chloe's amazement, even her very valid concerns about her parents had been duly considered by her boss and then swiftly and satisfactorily smoothed away.

She'd been stunned when he'd asked last night if he could visit her parents. She'd tried to protest. 'Sorry, no. Mum and Dad will be in bed already.'

'Why don't you ring them to check?' he'd said confidently.

To Chloe's surprise, her mother and father were still up, watching *Carols in the Cathedral* on TV, and, even more surprisingly, they said they'd be happy for her boss to call in, if he didn't mind finding them in their dressing gowns and slippers.

Zac said he didn't mind in the least.

'Chloe, there's sherry in the pantry and we can break open that box of shortbread you bought last week,' her mother suggested, sounding almost excited.

Zac had poured on the charm, of course, and, when it came to being charming, her boss was a genius. Even so, when he offered to put her parents up in the Riverslea Hotel, all expenses paid, with all their meals, most especially Christmas lunch, included, Chloe was sure they would refuse. It would be all too flash! They didn't like flashiness.

But, before her parents could object, Zac had thrown in a car with a driver to take them to church on Christmas Day, or to the doctor, or anywhere else they needed to go, and he'd offered to hire a nurse to check daily that they were keeping well and taking their correct medication.

Chloe's mother had looked a bit doubtful about this, until she'd received an elbow in the ribs from her dad.

'It would be like a holiday, love,' he'd said.

Still, Chloe had expected her parents to have second thoughts and say no. But then Zac also told them with commendable sincerity how extremely important, no, *invaluable,* their daughter was to him and how much he needed her for this very important mission in the UK.

Somehow he'd struck just the right note, which was

clever. If he'd praised Chloe to the skies, her parents would have been suspicious and he would have blown it.

Instead, by the time he'd finished, they were practically squirming with delight, like puppies getting their tummies rubbed just the way they liked it.

And now...this morning, her parents, with their out of date, simple clothes and humble, shabby luggage, including her dad's walking frame, had looked a trifle out of place in the luxurious hotel suite with thick white carpet, floor-length cream linen curtains, golden taps in the bathroom, not to mention panoramic views up and down the Brisbane River...but the grins on their faces had said it all.

'Chloe, you go and look after your nice Mr Corrigan,' they'd said, practically pushing her out of the door. 'Don't you worry about us.'

Chloe had closed her gaping mouth.

Remembering her parents' delight, she could almost imagine them exploring their hotel room like excited children, checking the little bottles of shampoo and bubble bath, flushing the loo and bouncing on the king-sized mattress. Zac Corrigan had achieved a minor miracle.

And Chloe was going to London!

Right. Deep breath. She only hoped she wasn't making a very serious mistake. After all, she knew why her boss had been so keen to avoid asking any of his female 'friends' to accompany him on this very personal journey. He liked to keep his relationships casual and this sojourn to London would be anything but casual.

Chloe also knew why her boss regarded her as a suitable choice. She was capable, conscientious and uncomplicated, and he trusted her to remain that way. Which suited her just fine. It did. Really.

Yes, there was a danger that those annoying long-ings she sometimes felt for Zac would surface, but she'd had plenty of practice at keeping them in check and she was sure she could survive his close proximity for a few short days.

So perhaps it was OK now to admit to herself that she was a tiny bit excited, or at least she would be if she wasn't concerned for Zac and the sad ordeal that still awaited him when they landed.

Eventually, they boarded and took off, making the long flight across Australia, and now they were, according to the map on the screen, flying high above the Indian Ocean...

The cabin lights were dimmed, Zac and Chloe had eaten an exquisite meal and had drunk some truly delicious wine, and their business class seats had been turned into beds.

Beside Chloe, her boss appeared to be asleep already, stretched out in jeans and a black T-shirt, with his shoes off and his belt removed and his feet encased in black and purple diamond-patterned socks. He had also plugged in earphones and was listening to music and he had slipped on the navy silk eyeshade the airline provided.

He was used to flying and she supposed he would sleep now, possibly for hours. He'd probably had very little rest during the previous night and she was sure he needed to sleep. Actually, Chloe's night had been sleepless as well, so she knew it would be sensible to try to follow his example. Otherwise, she'd end up in London, useless with jet lag, with a boss who was ready and raring to go.

Unfortunately, however, Chloe was too *wired* to sleep. The past twenty-four hours had been such a whirlwind and the thought of London was simply too exciting. She'd acquired her passport in happier times, when she'd thought she knew exactly where her life was heading...

But she'd never used it. So she'd never been on an international flight before, had never flown business class, and had certainly never been to England. It was hard to believe she would soon be seeing the famous Tower Bridge and Big Ben and Buckingham Palace.

Needing to calm down, she fished in her bag for the magazines she'd bought from the airport newsagent while Zac was busy with a phone call. The mags were all about mothers and babies and parenting and Chloe hoped to find an article or two about caring for newborns. Just in case...

Luckily, there were plenty of stories and columns covering all kinds of newborn issues. Chloe soon discovered what to do if a baby had colic, jaundice, an umbilical hernia...and masses of information about bath time, skin care, crying, feeding, burping...

She read the information conscientiously, trying to take it all in, wondering if she would actually be called on to apply any of this in practice and hoping she'd remember the important details. Her real-life experience of babies was limited to admiring her friends' offspring, and she'd found them cute to cuddle or play with and then she'd been happy enough to hand them back to their mothers.

After her life turned upside down several years ago, she'd given up her own dreams of motherhood, so she'd never given much thought to the finer details of green nappies or colic or projectile vomiting.

Even now, she blocked those images. Not every baby had those problems, surely?

Instead, Chloe allowed herself to picture a tiny, warm, sweet-smelling bundle in her arms, a dear little baby girl, with soft pink skin and perhaps dark hair like Zac's. A darling rosebud mouth.

'Aren't you sleepy?' murmured a deep voice beside her.

Startled, she turned to see that Zac had lifted his eyeshade and removed an earplug, and was watching her with marked curiosity.

Chloe's insides began to buzz—an annoying reaction to having him so close. 'I...er...thought it might help if I read for a bit first,' she said.

Zac leaned closer, frowning. 'What on earth are you reading?'

The magazine in her lap was unfortunately open at a full-page picture of a tiny baby attached to an enormous breast.

Chloe felt her cheeks heat. 'I...um...just thought...in case...you know, the baby...it would be handy to have a few clues.'

'It would indeed.' Zac spoke smoothly enough, but his eyes once again held the bleak shadows that had arrived with the terrible news about his sister. 'Good thinking, Ms Meadows.'

Chloe swallowed. It was more than a little unnerving to find herself lying so close to her boss's disconcerting, sad grey eyes. She could see his individual thick, dark eyelashes and the grainy texture of the skin on his jaw. She hadn't been this close to a man since—

'I'm sure I'll be sleepy soon,' she said quickly, before her thoughts could be hijacked by haunting memories.

'Tell me something you've learned,' Zac said, keeping his voice low so he didn't disturb the other passengers, many of whom were sleeping. 'I'm intrigued.'

'Something about babies?' Chloe whispered back.

He cast another glance at the photo in her lap. 'Or breasts, if you prefer.' He gave her a teasing smile.

Despite the rising heat in her cheeks, Chloe sent him a drop-dead look and closed the magazine.

'Babies then,' Zac amended, his lips still twitching in a smile. 'Tell me what you've learned about babies.'

In truth, she'd learned an awful lot that she hadn't really wanted to know—about a newly delivered mother's hormonal fluctuations, the stitches she might have in awkward places, her leaking or sore and swollen breasts.

'OK,' she said as she remembered a snippet of practical information that was safe to share with him. 'Did you know that you should wash the baby's bodysuits and nightgowns in hypoallergenic dye- and scent-free detergent?'

'Fascinating.' Zac yawned, clearly already bored.

Good, he might leave her in peace.

Chloe waited for him to replace his eye mask. Instead, he pointed to one of the magazines in her lap. 'Do you mind?'

This time, she didn't try to hide her surprise. 'You want to read one of these? A mother and baby magazine?'

Her corporate executive playboy boss could not be serious. The Zac Corrigan she knew wouldn't be caught dead with such an incriminating piece of reading material in his hands, not even in the relative anonymity of an international flight.

'Yes, please,' he said, holding out his hand and smiling blandly. 'I'd like to be educated.'

Lips compressed to stop herself from making a smart retort, Chloe handed him a magazine that focused on a baby's first six months. She supposed he was probably teasing her, but he might be trying to distract himself from thinking too much about his sister.

It was even possible that he genuinely wanted to learn. After all, if a father for Liv's baby couldn't be traced, Zac might soon find himself in complete charge of a newborn.

For a while they both read in peaceful silence, the small glow of their reading lights making golden cones in the otherwise darkened cabin. But Chloe couldn't relax. For one thing, she was too curious about how Zac might be reacting to the contents of his magazine.

But it wasn't long before he leaned close, speaking softly. 'Did you know that babies can stare at you while they sleep?'

'Excuse me?'

He smiled. 'It says here that they can sleep with their eyes half open. It looks pretty spooky, apparently.'

Although his smile, up close, was dangerous for Chloe's heart health, she couldn't help smiling back at him. 'Well, the article I'm reading warns that babies sometimes don't sleep at all.'

'No.' Zac feigned complete shock. 'That can't be right.'

'Well, I guess they sleep eventually, but some stay awake for much longer than they're supposed to.'

'A bit like us,' he said, looking around the business class cabin at all the other passengers, who appeared to be contentedly sleeping.

Chloe sighed. 'I guess we really should turn our lights out and try to sleep.'

'Yes, we should.' He closed the magazine and handed it back to her. 'Thanks for that. Most enlightening.'

By the time she'd stowed the magazines away, Zac had turned off his reading light, pulled down his eye-shade and folded his arms over his wide chest. 'Goodnight, Ms Meadows.'

He usually only addressed her this way when he was in a playful mood, which wasn't very often, mostly when he'd pulled off some extraordinarily tricky business coup. Chloe wondered if the playboy was coming out in him now, simply because he was lying beside a young woman who was close enough to touch and kiss.

That thought had no sooner arrived than her body reacted, growing warm and tingly and tight.

Oh, for heaven's sake.

Where had such a ridiculous reaction sprung from? Chloe gave herself a mental slap and glared at Zac.

'Goodnight, sir,' she said icily.

'And try to sleep.' He spoke without lifting his shade and he sounded now like a weary parent. 'We've a long way to go.'

Chloe didn't answer and she was relieved that she would not have to speak to her boss again until morning. She pulled on her own eye mask and tried to settle comfortably, hoping that the steady vibration of the plane and the hum of its engines would soothe her.

Her hopes were not realised.

She couldn't relax. She was too upset by her mental slip about kissing and touching her boss. Too busy delivering a good, stern lecture to herself. After all, she knew very well that Zac had asked her to accompany him on this trip precisely because he needed a female companion to whom he was *not* sexually attracted.

Her momentary lapse had no doubt been brought on by her over-tiredness. She knew nothing like *that* would happen. Zac had spent a good section of almost every working day in the past three years in her company without once trying to flirt.

Besides, she didn't want it to happen. She was far too sensible to ever fall for her boss's superficial good looks and charming wiles. Apart from the fact that she'd had her heart broken once and never wanted to experience that pain again, there was no way on this earth that she would allow her name to end up on the spreadsheet of his *Foolish Females*.

Unfortunately, her attempt to sleep only lasted about ten or fifteen minutes before she had to wriggle and fidget and try for a more comfortable position. Beside her, she heard a weary sigh. 'Sorry,' she whispered.

Zac lifted the eye mask again and pinched the bridge of his nose.

'Sorry,' Chloe said again. 'I disturbed you, didn't I?'

He shook his head. 'Not really.' He yawned. 'I'm dog-tired, but I have a feeling I'm not going to sleep tonight.'

'Do you normally sleep on long haul flights?'

'Eventually.'

She wondered if he couldn't stop thinking about his sister. Was he simply too upset to sleep? She wished she could help.

'I don't have any brothers or sisters,' she said tentatively.

Zac frowned.

'Sorry,' she said quickly, wincing at her third apology

in as many minutes. 'I just thought you might want to talk, but I shouldn't have—'

'No, no, it's OK.' He sighed again, and lay staring into space, apparently thinking...

Chloe waited, not sure what else to say.

'Liv was eight years younger than me,' he said quietly. 'When our parents died, she was only ten, so I felt more like her father at times.' His mouth was a grim downward curve. 'She was my responsibility.'

Chloe stared at him now as she tried to take this in. Was the poor man blaming himself for his sister's accident? Did he feel completely responsible? 'But you must have been very young, too,' she said.

'I was eighteen. An adult.'

Only just, by the skin of your teeth. 'How awful for you to lose both your parents so young.'

'Yeah,' he agreed with another sigh.

Chloe didn't like to ask, but her imagination was running wild. 'How did it happen, Zac? Was there an accident?'

He shrugged. 'We'll never know for sure. My parents were sailing somewhere in Indonesia when their boat just disappeared. My father was a geologist, you see, and my mother was a marine biologist and they were mad keen on science and exploration, always on the lookout for a new discovery. I suppose you'd call them nutty professors. Eccentrics.'

So they'd just disappeared...? Poor Zac. How terrible to have his parents simply vanish, to never know if they'd been taken by pirates, or capsized in a tropical storm, or drowned when their boat struck a coral reef...

'They—they couldn't be still alive, living on some jungle-clad island, could they?'

Zac's mouth tilted in a wryly crooked smile. 'I've played with that fantasy, too. But it's been seventeen years…'

Chloe couldn't imagine how awful it must have been for him—a mere eighteen years old and forced to carry on living without answers, just with terrible possibilities.

'Right from the start I was worried about Liv,' he said next. 'I couldn't bear to see her disappear into a foster home, so I applied to be her guardian. I dropped out of uni and got myself a job, so we could live together and I could look after her.'

'Goodness,' Chloe said softly, hoping she didn't sound as surprised as she felt.

Zac's lips curled unhappily. 'It was possibly the stupidest decision I ever made.'

'Don't say that. I think it was incredibly brave of you.'

She was stunned to realise that Zac had sacrificed his own goals to try to keep what was left of his family intact. All she'd ever known about his private life was the revolving door of lookalike leggy blonde girlfriends. He'd never seemed to really care about any of them beyond their sex appeal and she'd assumed the 'care factor' gene was missing from his DNA.

But it was clear to her now that he'd cared very deeply about Liv.

'I couldn't keep her on track,' Zac said, so softly Chloe almost missed it. 'Liv never really looked on me as a parent. She wouldn't accept me in a fathering role, so I had very little influence, I'm afraid. I think she was mad at our parents for disappearing the way they did and she saw me as an inadequate substitute. Before she was out of her teens she was into drinking and trying drugs. And then she was like a nomad, never wanting to settle. She didn't want to study and she would never stay in one job for long enough to get any real skills. She was like a butterfly, always searching for a brighter flower.'

'Might she have inherited that urge from your parents?'

'Quite possibly, I guess.'

He stared unhappily up at the cabin's ceiling and Chloe wished she could offer him wise words of consolation.

She did her best. 'Honestly, I don't think you should blame yourself for this accident, Zac.'

But he simply shook his head and closed his eyes.

It was ages before Chloe drifted off to sleep and when she woke a soft grey light filled the cabin and flight attendants were bringing around hot towels to freshen their hands and faces, as well as glasses of orange juice.

'Morning, sleepyhead.'

Zac's seat was already back in the upright position and he looked as if he'd been to the bathroom and washed and shaved.

Chloe yawned and hoped her hair wasn't too messy. In a minute she would follow his example and freshen up. 'What time is it?'

'Seven forty-five. That's Greenwich Mean Time, of course. If we were still at home it would be five forty-five in the evening.'

So…her parents had almost completed their first day in the hotel. Chloe hoped they were still enjoying themselves.

If she'd been in Brisbane, she would be putting the final touches to the office's decorations and making last minute checks about the drinks and ice.

'I hope you're not worrying about your parents.'

'No, I'm not.' She knew they were in good hands and she'd left the hotel desk, the hired nurse and the chauffeur with all the phone numbers and information they could possibly need. 'I was thinking about the office Christmas party tonight, actually.'

'Really, Chloe?' Zac was frowning at her now, although his eyes glinted with puzzled amusement.

'I was looking forward to the party,' she admitted, no longer caring if this revealed her inadequate social life.

'You were looking forward to watching half the office staff get plastered and then staying behind to clean up their mess?'

She opened her mouth to protest.

Zac's smile was gently teasing. 'You're going to see London at Christmas. I promise you that's a thousand times better than the office do.'

'I suppose it would be. When should we get our first glimpse of England?'

'Oh, in about an hour.'

CHAPTER THREE

IT WAS RAINING when they touched down at Heathrow, but somehow that couldn't dim Chloe's excitement. As business class passengers with only carry-on baggage, she and Zac didn't have to hang around in long queues and soon they were outside, suddenly very grateful for their warm overcoats and scarves.

While they waited for a taxi she made a quick phone call to her parents.

'We're about to go down to the dining room,' her mum told her excitedly. 'We've already checked out the menu and we're having lamb cutlets and then rhubarb crumble. Give our love to Zac.'

They were having the time of their lives and, within moments, Chloe was climbing into a proper shiny black London taxi and her excitement mounted as they whizzed along busy rain-slick streets filled with other taxis and cars and bright red double-decker London buses. Ahead, on a pedestrian crossing, people huddled beneath umbrellas glistening with rain.

Zac asked the taxi driver to stop at their hotel to leave their luggage and Chloe caught a brief impression of huge glass doors, massive urns filled with greenery and enormous gold-framed mirrors in a white marbled foyer.

'Now, we'd better head straight to the Metropolitan Police,' Zac said when he returned.

'Yes.' Chloe dug out her phone and checked the arrangements she'd made for Zac to meet with Sergeant Davies. She gave their driver the address and then they were off again.

Three blocks later, they had stopped at traffic lights when she saw the trio of soldiers. The tall, broad-shouldered men were simply standing and chatting as they waited to cross a road, but all it took was the sight of their camouflage uniforms and berets to bring back memories of Sam.

It could still happen like that, even though she'd had three and a half years to recover. The smallest trigger could bring the threat of desperate black grief.

Not now...I can't think about him now...

But now, on the far side of the world with her handsome boss, this painful memory was a timely reminder of the heartache that came with falling in love. Chloe knew she had to be super-careful...and she was grateful she'd trained herself to think of Zac as nothing but her boss...glad that she'd become an expert at keeping a tight lid on any deeper feelings...

At the police station, Sergeant Davies was very solicitous as he ushered them into his office. He told them that Liv's death had been clearly accidental and there was no reason to refer it to the coroner.

'The young man who was driving your sister to the hospital is definitely in the clear,' he added. 'He's a Good Samaritan neighbour. He was injured, but he's going to be OK. A badly broken leg, I believe.'

Zac sat stiffly, his face as grim as granite, as he received this news.

'We'll be laying serious charges against the driver of the other car,' the sergeant then told them.

'Driving under the influence?' Zac asked.

This was answered by a circumspect nod of assent.

Zac sighed and closed his eyes.

Outside, Chloe wanted to suggest that they found somewhere for a coffee. She was sure Zac could do with caffeine fortification, but perhaps she shouldn't have been surprised that he was determined to push on with his unhappy mission. At work he always preferred to confront the unpleasant tasks first. It was one of the things she'd always admired about him.

Within moments of hitting the pavement, he hailed another taxi and they were heading for the cold reality of the Royal London Hospital.

Once there, Zac insisted on seeing his sister, but as Chloe watched him disappear down a corridor, accompanied by a dour-looking doctor in a lab coat, she was worried that it might be a mistake. Her fears were more or less confirmed when Zac returned, white-faced and gaunt, looking about ten years older.

She had no idea what to say. There was no coffee machine in sight, so she got him a drink of water in a paper cup, which he took without thanking her and drank in sips, staring at the floor, his eyes betraying his shock.

Eventually, Chloe couldn't bear it. She put an arm around his shoulders and gave him a hug.

He sent her a sideways glance so full of emotion she felt her sympathetic heart swell to bursting. He offered her a nod, as if to say thanks, but he didn't speak. She was quite sure he *couldn't* speak.

For some time they sat together, with their overcoats

bundled on the bench beside them, before one of the hospital staff approached them, a youngish woman with bright red hair. 'Mr Corrigan?'

Zac lifted his gaze slowly. 'Yes?'

The woman's eyes lit up with the predictable enthusiasm of just about any female who met Zac. 'I'm Ruby Jones,' she said, holding onto her bright smile despite his grimness. 'I'm the social worker looking after your case.'

'Right. I see.' Zac was on his feet now. 'I guess you want to speak to me about the…the child?'

'Yes, certainly.' Ruby Jones offered him another sparkling smile, which Chloe thought was totally inappropriate. 'Am I right in imagining that you'd like to meet your niece?'

'Meet her?' Zac looked startled.

'Yes, she's just on the next floor in the maternity ward.'

'Oh, yes, of course.' He turned to Chloe. 'You'll come, too, won't you?'

'Yes, if you like.'

Ruby, the social worker, looked apologetic. 'I'm afraid—in these situations, we usually only allow close family members into—'

'Chloe is family,' Zac intervened, sounding more like his usual authoritarian self.

Chloe stared at the floor, praying that she didn't blush, but it was a shock to hear Zac describe her as family. She knew it was an expedient lie, but for a crazy moment her imagination went a little wild.

'I'm sorry.' Ruby sounded as flustered as Chloe felt. 'I thought you mentioned a PA.'

Zac gave an impatient flick of his head. 'Anyway, you couldn't count this child's close family on two fingers.' He placed a commanding hand at Chloe's elbow. 'Come on.'

Chloe avoided making eye contact with Zac as the social worker led them to the lift, which they rode in silence to the next floor.

'This way,' Ruby said as they stepped out and she led them down a hallway smelling of antiseptic, past doorways that revealed glimpses of young women and bassinets. From all around were sounds of new babies crying and, somewhere in the distance, a floor polisher whined.

Zac looked gloomy, as if he was hating every minute.

'Have you ever been in a maternity ward before?' Chloe asked him out of the side of her mouth.

'No, of course not. Have you?'

'Once. Just to visit a friend,' she added when she saw his startled glance.

Ahead of them, the social worker had stopped at a glass door and was talking to a nurse. She turned to them. 'If you wait here at this door, we'll wheel the baby over.'

Zac nodded unhappily.

Chloe said, 'Thank you.'

As the two women disappeared, Zac let out a heavy sigh. His jaw jutted with dismal determination as he sank his hands deep into his trouser pockets. Chloe was tempted to reach out, to touch him again, to give his elbow an encouraging squeeze, but almost immediately the door opened and a little trolley was wheeled through.

She could see the bump of a tiny baby beneath a pink blanket, and a hint of dark hair. Beside her, she heard her boss gasp.

'Oh, my God,' he whispered.

The trolley was wheeled closer.

'So here she is.' The nurse was middle-aged and hearty and she gave Zac an encouraging smile. 'She's a proper little cutie, this one.'

Chloe couldn't help taking a step closer. The nurse was right. The baby was incredibly cute. She was sound asleep and lying on her back, giving them a good view of her perfectly round little face and soft skin and her tiny nose—and, yes, her perfectly darling rosebud mouth—just as Chloe had imagined.

The baby gave a little stretch and one tiny hand came out from beneath the blanket, almost waving at them. There was a hospital bracelet around her wrinkled wrist. Chloe saw the name Corrigan written on it and a painful lump filled her throat.

Zac was staring at the baby with a kind of awestruck terror.

'So what do you think of your niece, Mr Corrigan?' asked Ruby, the social worker.

He gave a dazed shake of his head. 'She's tiny.'

'Her birth weight was fine,' the nurse said, sounding defensive, as if Zac had directly criticised her hospital. 'At least seven pounds.'

The social worker chimed in again. 'Would you like to hold her?'

Now Zac looked truly horrified. 'But she's asleep,' he protested, keeping his hands rammed in his pockets and rocking back on his heels as if he wished he could escape. For Chloe, by contrast, the urge to pick the baby up and cuddle her was almost overwhelming, as the maternal yearnings that she'd learned to suppress came suddenly rushing back.

She saw a frowning look exchanged between the nurse and the social worker and she worried that this was some kind of test that Zac had to pass before they could consider handing the baby into his care.

'Go on,' Chloe urged him softly. 'You should hold her for a moment. You won't upset her. She probably won't even wake up.'

Zac felt as if the air had been sucked from his lungs. He couldn't remember when he'd ever felt so out of his depth. The nurse was peeling back the pink blanket to reveal a tiny baby wrapped tightly in another thinner blanket. This was going to happen. They were going to hand her to him and he couldn't back out of it.

'Our little newborns feel safer when they're swaddled firmly like this. It also makes them easier to hold,' the nurse said as she lifted the sleeping bundle.

Reluctantly, Zac drew his hands from his pockets and hoped they weren't shaking.

'Just relax,' the nurse said as she placed the baby in his arms.

Relax? She had to be joking. It was all right for her. She did this every day. He was still getting over the agony of seeing Liv. And now he was so scared he might drop her baby...

She was in his arms.

He could feel the warmth of Liv's baby reaching him through the thin wrap. Could feel her limbs wriggling. Oh, dear God, she was so real. Alive and breathing. He forced himself to look down into her little pink face, so different from the deathly white one he'd so recently witnessed...

And yet...the similarity was there...

He found it so easily in the baby's soft dark hair, in

the delicate curve of her fine dark eyebrows, and in the tiniest suggestion of a cleft in her dainty chin.

'Oh, Liv.'

His sister's name broke from him on a desolate sob. His vision blurred as his throat was choked by tears.

Chloe's heart almost broke when she saw the silver glitter in Zac's eyes.

Even now, under these most difficult circumstances, it was a shock to see her boss cry. Zac was always so in control. In the day-to-day running of his business, it didn't matter how worried or upset or even angry he was, he never lost his cool. Never.

He usually viewed any kind of trouble as a challenge. In fact, there were days when he seemed to thrive on trouble and conflict. Twice, to her knowledge, he'd taken his company to the very brink of economic peril, but he'd never lost his nerve and had emerged triumphant.

Of course, there was a huge gulf between the challenges of the business world and a personal heartbreaking tragedy.

Now Zac Corrigan, her fearless boss, was caught in the worst kind of heartbreak and he was shaking helplessly as tears streamed down his face.

'Here,' he said, thrusting the baby towards Chloe. 'Please, take her.'

Her own emotions were unravelling as she hastily dumped their coats to accept the warm bundle he pressed into her arms. The poor man had been through so much—*too* much—in such a short time and, on top of everything else, he was dealing with jet lag. But, even though he had every reason to weep, Chloe knew he would be mortified to break down like this in public.

She wasn't at all surprised when Zac turned from them and strode back down the corridor, his head high and his shoulders squared as he drew deep breaths and fought for composure.

Watching him, she held the baby close, inhaling the clean and milky smell of her. She thought how perfectly she fitted in her arms.

Beside her, Ruby, the social worker, said, 'It's such a very sad situation.'

Indeed, Chloe agreed silently.

The baby squirmed now and beneath the blanket she gave a little kick against Chloe's ribs. Chloe wondered if this was how it had felt for Liv when she'd been pregnant. *Such a short time ago.*

Oh, help. If she allowed herself to think about that, she'd start weeping, too.

Perhaps it was just as well that she was distracted by Zac's return. He seemed sufficiently composed—although still unnaturally pale.

'I'm so sorry for your loss,' the nurse said.

Zac held up a hand and gave a brief nod of acknowledgement. 'Thank you.' His manner was curt but not impolite. Then he said, in his most businesslike tone, 'I guess you need to bring me up to speed.' He shifted his now steady gaze to the social worker. 'What's the current situation? Has anyone been able to locate the father?'

Ruby shook her head. 'I'm afraid we've had no luck at all.'

'You've definitely ruled out the fellow who was in the car with Liv?'

'Yes.'

At this news, Zac looked bleaker than ever.

'We've also interviewed the people who lived in the

share house with your sister,' Ruby said next. 'But they haven't been able to help us. They said Olivia wouldn't tell anyone the father's name. She simply told them that he wouldn't be interested in a child and she didn't want anything more to do with him.'

Zac stared at her for a long moment, his grey eyes reflecting a stormy mix of emotions. Eventually he nodded. 'That sounds like my sister, I'm afraid. But there was a boyfriend. I'm pretty sure Liv was still with him last Christmas. An Australian. A singer in a band.'

'Bo Stanley?'

Zac nodded grimly. 'Yes, I'm pretty sure that's his name.'

Again, she shook her head. 'A housemate did mention him and he's still in the UK, so we made contact and had him tested. It was easy to disqualify him. He's completely the wrong blood type.'

This time, Zac stared at her as if he was sure she had to be mistaken, but eventually he gave an unhappy shake of his head and shrugged. 'I guess he's off the hook, then.'

In Chloe's arms, the baby gave a little snuffling snort. When Chloe looked down she saw that her eyes had opened. The baby blinked and stared up at Chloe, straight into her eyes.

How much could those newborn dark grey eyes see? The baby's expression was definitely curious. Trusting, too. Her intense, seemingly focused gaze pierced Chloe's heart and she was enveloped by a rush of warmth, a fierce longing to protect this tiny, sweet girl. *It would be so easy to love her.*

She realised that Zac was watching her.

His gaze lingered on her as she stood there with the

baby in her arms. Surprise flared in his eyes and then a softer emotion. Chloe held her breath and for a winded moment her mind played again with hopelessly ridiculous possibilities…

Fortunately, Zac quickly recovered. 'OK,' he said, looking quickly away and becoming businesslike again. 'I guess my next question is about the baby.'

'What would you like to know?' the nurse asked guardedly.

'Is she healthy?'

'Perfectly.' She sniffed as if his question had offended her. 'You would have been informed before now if there was a problem.' Then, more gently, she asked, 'Do you have a particular concern?'

Zac grimaced uncomfortably. 'My sister had a drug habit, or at least she used to.' He shot a quick glance to Chloe and then looked away, as if he was embarrassed to have his employee hear this admission. 'It was some time back,' he added quickly. 'And Liv assured me she's been clean ever since, but I assume you've run the necessary tests?'

'Yes, Mr Corrigan. I can reassure you there were no signs that the baby has been adversely affected by alcohol or drugs.'

'Well, that's good news at least.' He swallowed. 'So…' Looking from the nurse to the social worker, he summoned a small smile, a glimmer of his customary effortless charm. 'What's next?'

Ruby, the social worker, was clearly surprised. 'Well…as you're next of kin and you've been named as guardian—'

'Yes, I've brought a copy of my sister's will if you need to see it.'

'And you've come all the way from Australia,' Ruby continued. 'I—I mean *we* were assuming that you planned to care for the baby.'

Zac nodded and his throat worked as he swallowed again.

Chloe knew he felt overwhelmed. He'd fielded successive shocks in the past twenty-four hours and she felt compelled to speak up. 'We've only just arrived from Heathrow and Mr Corrigan hasn't had any time to adjust, or to buy any of the things the baby will need.'

The nurse nodded. 'Of course. I understand.'

Shooting Chloe a grateful look, Zac added, 'If the baby could remain in your care for a little longer, I'd be happy to pay for any additional costs.'

This could be arranged, they were told, and Zac was also given a list of funeral parlours, as well as the name and address of Liv's share house, so that he could collect Liv's belongings. On that sobering note, they departed.

Outside the hospital a brisk December wind whipped at them, lifting their hair and catching at the ends of their scarves. Standing on the footpath on Whitechapel Road, Zac almost welcomed the wind's buffeting force and the sting to his cheeks. He dragged in an extra deep lungful of chilled air, as if it might somehow clear the raw pain and misery that roiled inside him. But there was no way he could avoid the two images that kept swimming before his vision. The pale, bruised, lifeless face of his beautiful sister and the small, red, but very much alive face of her tiny newborn daughter.

His niece.

His new responsibility.

The frigid air seemed to seep into Zac's very blood

along with this chilling reality. This baby, this brand new human being had no other family. He was *it*. She would be completely dependent on him.

He shot a glance to Chloe, whose cheeks had already turned quite pink from the cold. The high colour made her look unexpectedly pretty and he thought how fabulous she'd been this morning. In fact, his decision to bring his PA with him to London had been a stroke of pure genius. On the long flight, at the police station and again at the hospital, Chloe's no-fuss efficiency and quiet sympathy had been exactly the kind of support he'd needed.

'I vote we go back to the hotel now,' he said. 'We can check in and get a few things sorted.'

Chloe nodded. 'I'll check out those funeral parlours, if you like. It might be hard to find a—a place—with Christmas and everything.'

Zac was about to agree, but then he remembered the heartbreaking decisions he might be required to make. 'I'd better talk to them, Chloe. Anyway, you're probably exhausted.'

'I feel fine, actually.' She smiled. 'Being outside and grabbing a breath of fresh air makes all the difference.'

You're a breath of fresh air, he almost told her, and then thought better of it. Even minor breaches of their boss-PA boundaries seemed to make Chloe uncomfortable and now that she'd given up her Christmas and had come all this way, he didn't want to upset her. Instead he said, 'And I'll also make contact with the share house people.'

'Yes, it might be worth finding out what Liv's already bought before you start shopping.'

Zac frowned. Suddenly, his mega-sensible PA wasn't making any sense at all. 'Shopping?'

'For the baby.'

'Oh.' He gulped nervously. 'Yes, of course.'

A vision of a mountain of nappies and prams and tins of formula mushroomed in Zac's imagination. He felt overwhelmed again as he raised a hand to hail their taxi.

In a matter of moments, they were heading back into the city centre. Chloe leaned back in the seat and closed her eyes. She was probably worn out, even though she'd denied it. Zac had never seen her like this—with her eyes closed, her dark lashes lying softly against her flushed cheeks, her lips relaxed and slightly open.

She looked vulnerable and he found his attention riveted…

This wasn't the first time he'd entertained the idea of kissing Chloe, of making love to her, but, just as he had on the other occasions, he quickly cut off the thought.

From the start, when he'd first employed Chloe, he'd quickly recognised her value as his PA and he'd set himself clear rules. No office affairs. Ever.

Of course, there'd been times when he'd wished to hell that he wasn't so principled where Chloe was concerned. More than once they'd been deep in a business discussion when he'd been completely distracted by her quiet beauty, but it was almost certainly for the best that his common sense had always prevailed.

And now, once again, Zac dismissed ideas of tasting her softly parted lips and he wrenched his thoughts back to his new responsibilities.

A tiny baby…such an alarming prospect for a commitment-shy bachelor. If he took Liv's little daughter into his care, she would rely on him for everything—for food, for shelter, clothes…love. As she grew older she would look up to him for wise guidance, for entertainment, for security. She would require vast amounts of his time and patience.

No doubt she would view him as her father.

Her daddy…

The thought brought shivers fingering down Zac's spine. He couldn't deny he'd been hoping that the baby's biological father would emerge and make a claim, but he'd also been worried by the prospect. Knowing Liv, the guy was bound to be a no-hoper. Now, the possibility of a father galloping up on a white charger to save the day was fast disappearing and this left Zac with a different, but equally worrying set of problems…centring on his own, very real inadequacies…

He was very aware that his personal life was at best… haphazard…but there was a good reason for that—in more recent years he'd been making up for lost time.

Liv had been so young when their parents died, and for many years Zac had made her his first priority. He'd juggled several part-time jobs so that he could be at home for as much of Liv's out-of-school time as possible.

It was only *after* Liv had turned eighteen and struck out on her own, that he'd decided he might as well have some fun, so when it came to dating women he'd been a late starter. By then he'd also discovered he had a head for business as well as a talent for attracting gorgeous girls. He'd enjoyed the combination of work and play so much that he hadn't felt a need to settle down.

Now…as he stared out at the busy London traffic, at the towering modern buildings and the occasional ancient stone church hunkering within the skyscraper forest, he wondered if adoption might be the best option for Liv's baby.

It wasn't the first time Zac had toyed with the idea. Ever since the first shocking phone call from London , the possibility of adoption had been there, nagging at the back of his thoughts.

A huge part of him was actually quite willing to hand the baby over, and not because he was keen to shirk his responsibility, but because he was so totally scared of failure. With Liv, he'd tried his damnedest and he'd failed spectacularly, so how could he hope to be any more successful with her baby?

And yet…

Zac dragged an agonised hand over his face as guilt squirmed unpleasantly inside him. Could he really bring himself to hand that tiny bundle, that little 'mini-Liv', over to strangers?

After all, his sister had named him as guardian of her children in her will, and surely she wouldn't have made that weighty decision if she'd wanted her baby to be adopted.

Problem was…if the child was *not* adopted, there were very few alternatives. He certainly couldn't care for a baby on his own and he shuddered at the idea of a procession of housekeepers and babysitters and nannies.

He had to find a better solution. Fate had handed him a second chance to care for a member of his family and he simply *had* to get it right this time.

Liv's child needed security and continuity and she needed someone else besides him, someone who would balance his strengths and weaknesses. But a baby also needed someone who would really care about her and love her and, most importantly, stay with her…

What the poor kid needed was a mother...

With a heavy sigh, Zac closed his eyes, recalling a long ago image of Liv as a baby. He could picture their house in Ashgrove in a street lined with Bunya pines. Their mother was bathing Liv in a special little baby bath on the kitchen table, holding her carefully in the crook of her arm as she squeezed water from a facecloth over her fat little tummy.

Their mum had made a game of it and every time the water touched Liv's tummy, the baby would laugh and splash. Zac remembered the happiness of that squealing baby laughter, remembered the shining joy and impossible-to-miss love in his mother's face.

At the time he'd been a bit jealous and oh, so aware of the vital importance of a mother's love.

Oh, Liv, Liv...you should have been a mother, too.

Watching from the seat in the taxi beside Zac, Chloe saw his face twist with pain. He was looking away, out of the window, and he had no idea he was being observed. His mouth was trembling and then he grimaced and bit down hard on his lip as if to hold back a sob, and she could see tears again, could see the raw, agonising pain in his face. She longed to reach out, but she knew he would hate to be caught on the brink of breaking down yet again.

Still staring bleakly through the window, Zac's weary mind threw up a picture of Chloe at the hospital this morning. He remembered how perfectly the baby had fitted into the cradle of her arms, remembered the warm glow in Chloe's chocolate eyes as she looked down at her. He remembered the equally warm, melting sensation that he'd felt as he'd watched the two of them.

So natural and right…

Yes, there could be no question. What the baby needed most definitely, *absolutely*, was a mother.

And suddenly, arriving with the lightning jolt swiftness of every great idea, Zac discovered the perfect solution.

'You know what this means, don't you?' he announced in sudden triumph.

Beside him Chloe jumped and blinked as if she'd been woken from sleep. 'What?' She was frowning. 'Excuse me?'

'This baby,' Zac said impatiently. 'Liv's baby. There's only one way to take proper care of her.'

Despite Chloe's puzzled frown, her eyes widened with curiosity. 'What is it?'

'I'll have to take the plunge.'

'What plunge?'

'Into wedded bliss.' He tried to sound more excited. 'I'll have to get married.'

CHAPTER FOUR

MARRIED?

Zac Corrigan married?

Chloe stared at her boss, too stunned to speak. There was every chance she wasn't breathing and she had huge doubts about her hearing.

Surely she must have dreamt that Zac, the serial dater, truly wanted to get married?

He was watching her with a smile that didn't quite reach his worried eyes. 'Don't look so shocked,' he said.

She gave a dazed shake of her head, as if to clear it, and sat up straighter. 'Sorry. I think I must have nodded off and didn't hear you properly. What did you just say?'

'I've found the perfect solution to the baby problem.'

'Which is…?' she prompted cautiously.

Zac lifted his hands in a gesture of triumph, as if he was announcing the latest boost in company profits to a group of delighted shareholders. 'It's obvious that I need to get married.'

Good grief. She had heard him correctly.

For no more than a millisecond the word 'marriage' uttered by Zac Corrigan sent a strange thrill zinging through Chloe, skittering across her skin and lifting fine hairs. But, almost immediately, she came to her senses.

He was pulling her leg, of course. If she hadn't been so tired she would have seen the joke immediately.

'Marriage?' She laughed. 'Yeah, right.'

'I'm serious, Chloe.'

'Yes, of course you are.'

'I mean it.' He said this forcefully, as if he was growing impatient with her. 'It's the perfect solution.'

For some men, possibly, but not for you, Zac.

Clearly, jet lag had caught up with her devilishly handsome playboy boss. Jet lag plus too many personal shocks in a short space of time.

Unless...

Chloe supposed it was possible that Zac had fallen deeply in love very recently, without her knowing. 'I should have asked,' she said quickly. 'Do you already have a lucky lady in mind?'

Please, don't let it be that giggling girl who answered his phone the other evening.

Perhaps it was just as well that their taxi pulled up outside their hotel at that precise moment. Zac didn't answer Chloe's questions and the crazy conversation was dropped. Instead, he turned his attention to signing for the fare, making sure it included a generous tip.

Then a young man, resplendent in a uniform with tassels, opened the taxi door for Chloe. She had an almost film star moment as she went up the short flight of stone stairs with Zac to enormous glass doors, opened for them by another man in livery.

Once inside the glamorous high-ceilinged foyer with an exquisitely decorated soaring Christmas tree, they were greeted by more smiling staff who attended to the business of collecting their luggage and checking in.

It all went super-smoothly, with a level of service

that exceeded Chloe's experiences on previous business trips. She'd certainly never stayed anywhere this glamorous before.

Zac had interrupted her last Wednesday evening, when she'd been about to make the hotel booking.

'Hang on,' he'd said, as he hunted in his desk and produced a business card. 'Try this place. I stayed there once. It's central and rather good.'

It was much pricier than his usual budget, but Chloe hadn't liked to argue and now, here they were, in a lift with an intricately tiled floor and mirrored walls, taking them silently swishing upwards...

Seconds later, they were standing in the carpeted hallway outside their adjoining rooms. 'Take your time settling in,' Zac said. 'Perhaps you'd like to rest up for a bit?'

Chloe was tempted, but she knew it wouldn't be wise. 'If I fall asleep now, I'll probably find myself wide awake and prowling around at midnight.'

To her surprise, he responded with a sparkling-eyed, slightly crooked smile.

She frowned. 'Did I say something funny?'

'No, as always you were eminently sensible, Chloe, but I have a very curious imagination. I couldn't help playing with the idea of my Ms Meadows on a midnight prowl.'

To her dismay, her mind flashed an image of the two of them meeting out here in the corridor when she was wearing nothing but a nightie and heat flared as if Zac had struck a match inside her. 'Don't be ridiculous,' she snapped.

He wiped the smile, but irritating amusement still lurked in his grey eyes. 'Seriously, it's probably best if you can manage to stay awake until this evening. How about we meet in half an hour for lunch?'

'Sounds fine. Would you like me to make you a cup of tea, sir?' She added this in her most deferential manner, to remind them both of the very clear lines drawn between his status and hers.

Zac's response was another unsettling smile and, for a moment, he looked as if he was going to make yet another inappropriately playful remark, but then he gave a slight shake of his head and the amused light in his eyes died. 'No, thanks. I'll manage.'

Chloe was annoyed that she still felt unsettled as she slid the key in her lock and went into her room.

But she was soon distracted by the room's jaw-dropping gorgeousness. It had an enormous bed, a thick, pale carpet and comfortably padded armchairs, as well as vases of roses. Everything was in tasteful shades of pink and cream, and the view was beautiful, too, through elaborately draped windows to green English parkland with enormous ancient trees spreading winter-bare branches above smooth velvet lawns.

She set her bag down and took off her coat and scarf and laid them carefully on the end of the bed. She slipped off her shoes, and when her stockinged feet sank into the deep pile carpet she gave a blissful little twirl and then a skip.

She thought of her parents back in Brisbane, enjoying their lovely hotel stay, which was also courtesy of Zac. It seemed wrong somehow that both she and her parents were enjoying a luxurious and other-worldly experience for such a very sad reason.

Sobered by this thought, she located the tea-making facilities hidden discreetly behind white-painted doors.

Soon she had the jug boiled and a bag of Lady Grey tea brewing in a delicate china cup and, with milk and a half-teaspoon of sugar added, she took the cup to an armchair. For the first time in days, she had a little time to herself, to relax and unwind. But she couldn't stop thinking about her boss and the difficult phone calls he was making right next door.

As an only child, she didn't know what it was like to lose a sibling, but she knew all too well what it was like to lose someone she loved…and, without warning, she was swamped by memories.

Once again she was feeling the crushing weight of the raw grief caused by Sam's death. It had sent her retreating home to her elderly parents and, once there, their increasing age and health issues had become her excuse to withdraw from the pain of her old life…

Now, curled in the armchair, clutching the lovely cup to her chest, Chloe wept for Sam, her fiancé…and for her lost dreams…and also, in a more complicated way, she found herself weeping, as well, for her boss.

'Are you sure you're OK, Chloe? You're looking a little peaky,' Zac commented when they met again thirty minutes later.

She looked surprised. 'I'm perfectly fine, thanks.'

He might have quizzed her further, but he knew he probably looked rather pale and drawn, too. He'd certainly felt flattened after his discussions with the funeral director.

'Liv's share house is in Islington,' he said, referring to one of the other phone calls he'd made. 'It's probably just as easy to take the Tube and we can go out there first thing in the morning.'

Chloe nodded.

'I was hoping you'd come, too.'

'Yes, of course.'

The enormity of his relief was out of all proportion but, with that small issue settled, they headed for Oxford Street, hunting for a place to eat. Or at least that was Zac's plan until Chloe was completely captivated by the extravagant Christmas displays in the shops' windows.

He was patient enough while she admired them—blinding white snow scenes complete with pine trees and clever mechanical toys, glittering tables laden with sumptuous feasts, fantastic fashions displayed against a stunning snowy backdrop.

He knew the shop windows were incredibly inventive and artistic, but he found it difficult to enjoy them. He was finding it impossible to shake off the burden of his new and weighty responsibilities.

He'd been slightly miffed that Chloe had laughingly dismissed his brilliant solution of marriage without giving it so much as a moment's thought. He was also surprised she'd been so forthright. Usually, if his PA disagreed with him, she kept her opinions to herself, unless he specifically asked for her input.

Of course, he'd never discussed his private life with Chloe until now, but everything had changed last Wednesday evening. And it had changed again this morning when he saw his sister's tiny baby. He was overwhelmed anew by the huge pressure of his *duty*, and now, as Chloe turned from a clever display of robots made from children's building blocks, he was gripped by a new kind of urgency.

'You know, I'm at a loss about this child,' he said. 'I can't possibly care for her on my own.'

Perhaps he spoke a little too loudly. A woman rushing past them, laden with shopping parcels, sent Chloe
a distinctly disapproving glance.

Fortunately, Chloe ignored her and simply stepped
closer to Zac, lowering her voice. 'You can have all kinds
of help with a child, you know. There are nannies and—'

Zac cut her off in a burst of impatience. 'Nannies
come and go. I want—' He sent another glare to the
steady stream of Christmas shoppers flowing around
them and gave an impatient shake of his head. They
couldn't talk about this here, and the cafés in Selfridges
were bound to be packed at this time of the year.

'Come on.' He tugged at her coat sleeve. 'I've remembered a pretty good pub just around the corner.'

As Zac charged off, Chloe almost had to run to keep
up with him.

She soon forgave him, though, when he located the
pub. It had a very appealing wonderfully 'old English'
atmosphere created by small paned windows with white
trims, a green door and a window box spilling red, white
and purple petunias.

Inside, the dark, timber-panelled space was as warm
and cosy as the outside had promised. Appetising aro-
mas drifted from the kitchen, and there was a friendly
buzz in the room as diners, who were taking a break
from their Christmas shopping, chatted quietly at tables
covered in white linen.

Chloe and Zac took off their coats and scarves and
hung them near the door, which was quite a novel experience for Chloe after subtropical Brisbane, and a friendly
young waiter showed them to a table in a corner.

Several of the female diners turned and unashamedly

followed Zac with their eyes. Chloe was used to this, of course, but Zac hardly seemed to notice them.

As they made themselves comfortable, Chloe was tempted to relax completely and soak up the centuries-old atmosphere, but she was too conscious of the tension coming off Zac in waves. She wondered if he was still stewing over his crazy marriage idea. Surely he would soon wake up to himself?

At least he didn't try to raise the delicate subject until after they'd ordered. Chloe chose a Stilton and potato soup with a glass of white wine, while Zac ordered a beef and Guinness pie and half a pint of beer.

With that settled, Chloe decided that she should at least humour her boss. 'So are we still discussing this marriage plan, Zac?'

His grey eyes narrowed. 'On the assumption that you're prepared to be reasonable.'

'Of course I'll be reasonable, but you never did tell me if you had a future wife in mind.'

'Well…no.' He smiled a little ruefully. 'I'll admit that's a problem.'

Chloe stomped on the ridiculous flush of relief that swept through her.

'But I'm still quite sure marriage is the perfect solution.'

'Because…?'

'The baby will need a mother,' Zac said simply.

Ah, yes…

In a heartbeat, Chloe was remembering the sweet little bundle in her arms, the warm weight of Liv's baby, and she was reliving that amazing moment when she'd looked deep into the baby's bright little eyes and had felt her heart turn over.

The memory made her throat ache and she had to swallow before she could answer. 'Finding a mother would be the ideal solution,' she said, hoping the emotion didn't show in her face. 'But plenty of babies have been brought up by nannies.'

Ridiculous tears threatened and she looked away quickly to the end of the dining room. What on earth was the matter with her? She had to be very careful that she didn't become too emotionally caught up in Zac's problems. There was no point in becoming maudlin just because she'd given up her own dreams of a family when she'd gone home to her parents.

She turned her attention to the far wall, where a huge mantelpiece lent the restaurant a gracious Victorian air. With her gaze centred on it, she said lightly, 'Wasn't the British Empire practically raised by nannies in its heyday?'

Zac's jaw stiffened, a clear sign that he was annoyed. 'Let's stick to the twenty-first century.'

She tried again, in placating tones. 'I believe the modern nannies are very well trained.'

'But no nanny these days is going to stick with a child until she's an adult.'

'That might be a stretch.' Across the table, Chloe eyed her boss boldly. 'Then again, modern marriages don't always last very long either.'

A stubborn light gleamed in Zac's eyes as he stared unblinkingly back at her. 'I still think marriage is the most sensible option. I want this child to have stability, parents who'll stick around, perhaps a little brother or sister—a life as close to normal as possible.'

Such an alluring picture...

Chloe took a deep breath. Zac wanted to give the

baby everything Liv had lost.He wanted this quite badly, and desperate times required desperate measures. 'You have to do what you think is right, Zac. It's none of my business, anyway.'

'Actually…that's not quite true…'

Her heart began a frantic hammering. What did he mean?

'I thought you might be able to help me,' Zac said.

'Really? How?'

'You have that spreadsheet. We could go through it together—take another look at the possibilities.'

The spreadsheet… It was so ridiculous to feel disappointed in him. Why on earth might she have thought…?

'Please tell me you're joking,' she said quickly.

'I'm not. I'm deadly serious.'

'But trawling for a wife through a database is so—' *So wrong on so many levels.* 'So unromantic.' Chloe had to look away again.

She was remembering the day Sam proposed. They'd been walking in the rain along a cliff top, with the sea crashing and foaming on the rocks below. Sam had produced a ring and he'd actually gone down on one knee. It was *so-o-o-o* romantic. He'd told her how madly he loved her and their kiss in the rain had been the most exciting moment imaginable…

'I mean,' Zac was saying. 'For all we know, these modern marriages might fail for the very reason that they're based on romantic notions instead of common sense and logic.'

'So what are you saying now, Zac? That you don't believe in romance?'

Before he could respond, the waiter approached with their drinks.

'Meals won't be long,' the young man said cheerfully.

Zac thanked him and, as the waiter left, he raised his glass and smiled. 'Anyway…here's to you, Chloe Meadows, best PA ever.'

It was such a sudden turnabout, she knew she looked flustered and was possibly blushing. Again.

'I'm extremely grateful to you for agreeing to come here at such short notice,' Zac went on. 'And at such a difficult time of the year.'

As they clinked glasses, his smile was so sincere that Chloe gave a little laugh to cover her reaction.

'How could I turn down an all-expenses-paid trip to London?' she said, but she was actually wondering how Zac could be so exasperating one moment and then so charming the next.

After a sip of wine, which was exceptionally fine, she veered back to their previous discussion. Now that Zac had raised the thorny subject of marrying someone with the aid of a computer spreadsheet, it was like a prickle buried in her skin that she had to dig out. 'So I take it you don't believe in romance?' she challenged him again.

He shrugged. 'I think romance is problematical. I don't see how people can make a decision that lasts a lifetime based purely on their feelings. It's highly possible that there would be more successful marriages if everyone took a more practical approach.'

'Like arranged marriages?'

'Why not? They seem to work quite well in many cultures.'

Chloe took a deeper sip of her wine as she considered this. She had to admit it was true that arranged marriages often worked. Her parents' neighbours from Afghanistan were prime examples. The Hashimis' marriage had been arranged by their parents when they were still in their teens and they'd been happily together for forty years. In fact, Mr Hashimi seemed more devoted to his wife than ever.

'You know, you're *almost* making sense,' she said. 'Except—'

'Yes?' Zac prompted eagerly, but then the waiter appeared again with their meals.

Chloe was grateful for the interruption. She'd been about to say that she couldn't imagine many Australian women falling for Zac's scheme, but then she'd remembered the names in the list of his *Foolish Females* and she knew that quite a few of those girls would probably leap at the chance to marry her boss. After all, Zac Corrigan was exceptionally eligible.

'So it sounds as if you'd like to approach this marriage like a business strategy?' she said instead as she sprinkled croutons over her soup.

Zac nodded as he cut into his crusty pie to reveal rich dark meat and gravy. 'As a starting point, at least.'

'And how would you make your choice? Draw up a list of the attributes you want in this wife? Then try to find the perfect match from the *Fool*—from the list of girls you've already dated?'

'Exactly,' he said with a grin. 'I knew you'd come on board.'

An hour later, they were still in the pub.

Having finished their meals and drinks, they were onto their second cups of coffee, hoping to keep jet lag at bay for a little longer, and Chloe, to her own amazement, was helping to draw up Zac's list of wifely qualities.

'OK, let's see what you have so far.' She read from the

notes she'd typed into her phone. 'We—I mean *you*—
want someone who's sensible—' She'd been majorly
surprised that this had headed his list. 'Smart, sympathetic, reliable, has a sense of humour, likes kids, is not
too loud…'

Zac nodded. 'That sounds about right.'

What about size eight and blonde? This described
most of the girls he liked to date, but somehow Chloe
restrained herself from asking this and took a kinder approach. 'I don't think you really need a database, Zac.
You must already know which of your girlfriends has
these qualities.'

A deep frown furrowed his brow as he stared at his
coffee cup. 'It's hard to find them all in one person,
though, isn't it?'

When he looked up, he seemed genuinely perplexed.
'Angie Davis has a great sense of humour and she's probably good with kids, but I'm not sure she's all that reliable. And Sasha Franks would run a terrific household,
but she's a bit…cold.'

'What about Marissa Johnson?' Of all Zac's girlfriends, Chloe had liked Marissa the best. She was a
very friendly young woman who worked in a sports
store on the Gold Coast, and she had short dark hair and
a natural, make-up-free glow of the outdoors about her,
which made her a little different from his usual choices.

Zac, however, was shaking his head. 'Why does Marissa's name keep cropping up? You told me to invite her
here to London and I said no then.'

Chloe shrugged. 'I just think she's really nice, the
sort of girl I could be good friends with.' She smiled
sheepishly.' But I don't suppose that's helpful to you.'

'Actually, you're probably right about Marissa.' He

sighed heavily. 'But of all the girls I know, she's prob-ably the least likely to be interested in marrying me.'

'Are you sure?'

He nodded. 'I'm afraid I stuffed things up with her. I...er...kind of forgot to mention that I was still seeing someone else.'

Chloe groaned. 'For heaven's sake, Zac.'

He shrugged. 'The other girl was in Melbourne and it was only ever occasional, but Marissa still gave me the boot.'

Good for her, Chloe thought, but she kept the thought to herself. Instead, she found herself saying, 'You never know, she might forgive you if you asked very nicely. Putting a ring on her finger could make a world of dif-ference.'

She wished she felt happier about offering that last piece of unasked-for advice. It didn't help that Zac's re-sponse was a gorgeously brooding smile that made her wonder what he was thinking.

Was he actually in love with Marissa?

Why should I care? It's not as if I want him for my-self. Chloe knew she was far too sensible to make such a foolish mistake.

'I've never actually asked about *your* credentials,' Zac said suddenly.

'Mine?' A zap, like an electric spark, shot through Chloe. 'Wh-what d-do you mean?'

'Well, here I am seeking your advice and I don't even know if you're qualified. I know nothing about your social life. You're such a private girl, Chloe. I've never heard you mention going on a date.' He was looking at her now as if she was a very amusing riddle. 'For example…is there a boyfriend I should have apologised to when I dragged you away at Christmas?'

Chloe gulped. 'No—there's…er…no one at the moment.'

'You're a lovely girl…so there must be an explanation.'

Stifling her delight at his use of the word 'lovely', she decided that she wouldn't tell him about Sam. How could a man who didn't believe in romance possibly understand her pain, or why she'd retreated so completely from the dating scene?

Zac was still smiling, but the expression in his grey eyes was piercing now. It seemed to skewer her. 'You're not going to share that explanation, are you?' he said.

'No, I'd rather not.'

He frowned and, for the longest time, he regarded her with a look that was unexpectedly sympathetic, but, to Chloe's intense relief, he dropped the subject.

They walked back to their hotel through the gathering gloom of a wintry London afternoon. Street lights had already come on and the window displays made eye-catching splashes of colour.

Zac was beginning to feel a little better after a warming meal and a reasonably profitable chat with Chloe, as if he'd been trapped in a nightmare but was gradually finding his way out. He would certainly give the Marissa option more careful thought.

'I suppose you might have to think of a name for the baby,' Chloe said suddenly when they were about a block from their hotel.

'A name?' With a soft groan, Zac threw back his head

and stared helplessly up at the dark lowering clouds. 'I wouldn't have a clue where to begin.'

'Oh, I'm sure you'll have fun once you get started, Zac. There are so many pretty girls' names.'

'I guess.' But when he tried to think, he could only think of past girlfriends' names and he didn't want any of them. Beyond these, however, his mind drew a blank. 'Do you have any suggestions?'

Chloe laughed. 'Where do I start? Mind you, I'm no expert, but I think all the old classic names are still very popular—names like Emma and Sophie or Rose. Or, let me see, there's Isabella or simply Bella.'

'Bella's cute,' Zac admitted, thinking of the tiny pink-cheeked baby he'd been handed at the hospital.

'I guess you'd also want to choose something that went well with Corrigan.'

'Would I? Yes, I guess…'

'For example, Chloe Corrigan would sound a bit off.'

Inexplicably, Zac's chest tightened. 'Would it?'

'Definitely,' Chloe said gruffly. 'Too many Cs and Os. Although Kate or Katy might work. Katy Corrigan sounds catchy. Or maybe something pretty starting with M like Megan or Molly or Mia—or, if you wanted to be modern, you could go for something like Mackenzie.' His PA was obviously warming to this task.

'Molly,' Zac said quickly. 'I don't mind that. I don't know why, but the baby sort of looks like a Molly, doesn't she?'

Chloe turned to him. She was smiling, but her brown eyes were so soft and warm with emotion that the band around his chest pulled tighter.

'Molly's very cute,' she said. 'Or if you wanted to tie in a Christmas link, you could always go for Holly.'

'No, I'm warming to Molly,' Zac said. He liked to arrive at firm decisions. 'Molly Corrigan sounds all right, doesn't it? Or are there too many Os?'

'Molly's great.'

'Or Lucy. What about Lucy Corrigan? That sounds better, doesn't it?'

'Yes, Lucy's lovely,' Chloe said softly.

'Lucy Francesca Corrigan,' Zac refined, proud of his sudden inspiration.

'Oh, Francesca's gorgeous. What made you think of it?'

'It was my mother's name, although most people just called her Fran or Frannie.'

'It would be very fitting to name the baby after her grandmother. Lucy Francesca's so pretty. I love it!'

'Excellent. We can sleep on it and see if we still like it in the morning.'

For a moment, Zac thought he saw a glistening dampness in his PA's eyes, but she turned quickly to study another shop window, so he couldn't be sure.

He wondered if he'd said something wrong.

CHAPTER FIVE

ZAC WASTED NO time in getting to the share house the next morning. Having finally succumbed to jet lag on the previous evening, he and Chloe had opted to skip dinner in favour of much needed sleep and, consequently, they'd both woken early. A hearty hotel breakfast and a Tube ride later, they stood outside the house Liv had shared for the past twelve months.

Zac had no idea what to expect, but he wasn't totally surprised when his knock was answered by a girl with purple hair and a silver ring through her nose.

'Good morning,' he said rather formally. 'I spoke to someone called Skye on the phone.'

'Yeah,' the girl said. 'That's me.'

Zac lifted the empty suitcase he'd brought to collect Liv's belongings. 'I'm Zac Corrigan.'

Skye's face broke into an unexpectedly warm smile. 'Lovely to meet you, Zac.' She offered her hand, complete with black nail polish. 'Liv told us so much about you.'

'Really?' He couldn't hold back his surprise.

'Yeah, of course she did. She was dead proud of you, you know.'

But as she said this, her eyes filled with tears and—dammit—Zac felt his own eyes begin to sting.

'Come on in,' Skye said in a choked voice, blinking hard as she opened the door wider and stepped back to make room for them. 'Pete and Shaz have both left already for work.'

'We're not holding you up, are we?'

She shook her head. 'I don't work Saturdays.'

In the narrow hallway a faint smell of incense lingered. Zac introduced Chloe.

'Pleased to meet you.' Skye smiled now and regarded Chloe with interest. 'Are you Zac's girlfriend?'

'PA,' Zac and Chloe said together.

The girl gave a slightly puzzled frown, then shrugged and headed down the hall, nodding for them to follow.

'We miss Liv so much,' she said over her shoulder. 'But you must know that, Zac. You know what she was like. Such a live wire and always so lovely and kind.'

'Yes,' Zac said faintly as they entered the lounge room, which wasn't nearly as dilapidated as he'd expected.

The furniture was almost certainly second-hand and the sofa was draped in a hand-knitted shawl of red and purple wool, while the walls were hung with huge amateurish paintings in equally bright and gaudy oils. But everything was clean and tidy and the overall effect was surprisingly appealing. Artistic and cosy.

'Before I show you Liv's room,' Skye said, 'I thought I should mention that Father Tom dropped by last night.' Her eyes widened with the importance of this news. 'He said he could squeeze in a funeral on Monday morning, even though it's Christmas Eve...' The girl looked from Zac to Chloe. 'That is, if you'd like a church funeral.'

Zac hoped he didn't look as surprised as he felt. Avoiding Chloe's gaze, he asked, 'Did—did Liv attend church?'

'Oh, yeah.' The look Skye gave him was almost pitying. 'Every Sunday morning and on Wednesday evenings as well. We all go together. It's lovely.'

'Um…what kind of church?' he dared to ask.

'Oh, you can check it out for yourself, Zac. It's the little chapel around the corner. Father Tom's marvellous. You should see the work he does in the streets around here.'

'I see.' Zac swallowed. 'I'm afraid I had no idea about this. I've…er…made arrangements with a funeral director for a cremation.'

'But wouldn't you want a church service with Liv's friends as well?'

He realised he'd given no thought to the friends Liv might have made. She'd only been in England a year and he'd somehow pictured her wandering around with the guy from the band, pretty much alone and drifting…

Somewhat dazed, he looked Chloe's way and she immediately smiled and sent him an encouraging nod.

'A church service would be…perfect,' he said.

'Wonderful. I'll give Father Tom a ring, shall I?'

'Thank you.'

'Right. It's this way to Liv's room.' Skye was pointing. 'Feel free to take any or all of her things. Anything left, we can sort out.' Her voice wobbled and suddenly there were tears in her eyes again and her nose was distinctly pink. 'And stay as long as you like.'

'Thank you. You're very kind.' Still feeling dazed, Zac went to the doorway and then came to an abrupt halt when he saw his sister's room.

As a teenager, Liv's bedroom had always been a dive, with the bed unmade and clothes left lying on the floor where she'd climbed out of them, the waste basket overflowing with scrunched balls of paper and drink cans. For Zac, the messy room had been a constant battleground, but in the end he'd hated carrying on like an Army sergeant major and he'd given up trying to get her to tidy it.

In this room, the bed was covered by a smooth, spotless white spread and there was an arrangement of bright flowers in a vase on the bedside table. On top of a chest of drawers sat a small yellow teddy bear and neatly folded piles of baby clothing. Beside that a collection of toiletries…talcum powder and baby lotion and a glass jar filled with snowy cotton wool balls.

Taking pride of place in the corner stood a white bassinet of woven cane made up with clean sheets and with a soft pink blanket folded over one side, ready and waiting for a tiny occupant.

Stunned, Zac sagged against the doorpost.

The room said it all. His little sister had grown up and changed beyond recognition. Liv had found a true home here in London and she'd obviously been looking forward to motherhood. All evidence pointed to the fact that she'd planned to be a perfect mother, until fate cruelly robbed her of that chance, that *right*.

Without warning, he was swamped by a fresh deluge of sorrow and his chest swelled to bursting point as he felt his heart break all over again. He had no hope of holding back his tears.

It was a while later when he heard Chloe whisper softly behind him, 'Zac.'

He felt her hand on his arm, rubbing him through

his coat sleeve, and he found her touch unexpectedly comforting.

Straightening, he scrubbed a hand over his face. 'Sorry. I'm afraid I lost it again.'

'Oh, don't worry,' she said, swiping at her eyes. 'I've been blubbing, too.'

'It was such a shock.' He waved a hand at the room. 'I wasn't expecting this. Everything's so damn...*neat*.' He managed a broken laugh.

'It's charming,' Chloe said. 'Picture perfect.'

'The little monkey. Liv would never tidy a thing for me.'

They both laughed shakily, and stood looking about them. Then, drawing a deep breath, Zac set down the empty suitcase on a mat at the end of the bed. 'If only I had a clue where to start.'

Chloe crossed the room to the chest of drawers. 'I guess you'll definitely need these baby things.' She picked up the top item of clothing and held it out to him.

It was the tiniest singlet he'd ever seen. 'Wow, it's so little.'

'It's minuscule,' Chloe whispered, sharing his awe.

'I can't imagine trying to dress a wriggling baby in that,' Zac added with mild alarm.

Chloe smiled, but made no comment and he thought how lovely she looked. Actually...what man wouldn't be entranced by those shapely legs, that shiny, touchable hair? And how could he ignore the lovely warmth of her dark brown eyes? Bizarrely, in the midst of these saddest of circumstances, Zac found himself wondering why he'd always been so black and white about the boundaries he maintained with his PA.

'I'll get started, shall I?' she said, turning to open

the top drawer. 'I'm assuming you'll only take the baby clothes?'

'I think so.'

'There are plenty here. It looks like Liv was well prepared.'

Zac nodded and pledged to concentrate on the task at hand. 'If we set Liv's clothes to one side, Skye will know what to do with them.'

'But you'll want to keep things like this, Zac.'

'Like what?'

Chloe was holding out a small blue album. 'Take a look,' she said, sending him a significant glance.

It was a photo album, he quickly realised as he turned to the first page. It showed a professional photograph of his family taken in a studio when he was around ten.

His mother had used this photo to make a personalised Christmas card, he remembered. And there his mother was...looking youthful and beautiful with short dark hair and lively grey-green eyes, and wearing her favourite dress of tailored green linen.

Beside her, his father was wearing a white business shirt and dark trousers with a maroon tie. His father's hair had already started to grey at the temples, but his face was tanned from all the time he spent outdoors in the bush, tracking down the plants and animals that were endangered by extensive mining.

His mum had dressed them all in Christmas colours, so Zac was wearing a dark red polo shirt with pale chinos, while Liv, aged two, was in a white dress with a green and red tartan sash. Zac smiled, remembering how hard it had been to get Liv to sit still for the photo.

Now...they were all gone.

He was the only one left...and, suddenly, looking

at the photo was unbearable. He shut the album with a snap. He'd had more than enough heartbreak for one day.

Without speaking, he walked over to the suitcase and dropped the album into it. Chloe glanced at it and then up at him, but she didn't say a word. Her eloquent dark eyes told him that she understood. For that, he almost hugged her.

It was as they were leaving and thanking Skye yet again that Zac remembered to ask, 'Do you know if Liv had any names chosen for the baby?'

Skye laughed. 'She had hundreds. You should have seen the lists. Liv knew she was having a girl, of course.'

'Did she have a favourite name?'

'Not as far as I could tell. The name seemed to change almost every day. The only thing Liv was certain about was that she wanted her mother's name, Francesca, for the middle name.'

'Ah…' Zac caught Chloe's eye and they shared a smile and he felt an unexpected glow inside. It was incredibly reassuring to know that his first important decision about the baby had been on the right track.

'Are you going to check out the church?' Chloe asked when they were once again outside.

'Yes, good idea. I wouldn't mind meeting this Father Ted, too, if he's around.'

'Tom,' Chloe corrected. 'Father Tom.'

Zac grinned. 'Thanks, Ms Meadows. I suppose the chances of finding him on a Saturday morning are slim.'

They saw the tiny stone church as soon as they rounded the corner. Surrounded by a narrow fringe of green lawn, it was like a relic from the past, smack bang next to a row of brightly painted modern shops.

The front door of the church was open, offering an enticing glimpse of a nativity scene, complete with a stable and straw and a plaster donkey. When Zac and Chloe detoured around it, they found two women in the church's darkened interior, arranging white gladioli and bunches of holly in tall copper urns.

'I was hoping to find Father Tom,' Zac told the nearest woman.

She nodded towards a small wooden arch-shaped door in the far wall. 'Over there in the vestry.'

'Thank you.'

'He's very busy with Christmas and everything, and there'll be a wedding here in an hour or so.'

'I won't take up much of his time.'

As he turned to head off, Chloe held out her hand for the suitcase. 'I'll look after that.'

'OK, thanks.' Leaving Chloe sitting in a pew, Zac realised how quickly he'd become used to having her right beside him. *Almost as if...*

He cut off that thought before it distracted him from the task at hand.

At the vestry he gave two short knocks and the door was opened by a young sandy-haired fellow in jeans and a black knitted sweater.

'Hi there,' he said. 'How can I help you?'

'I was hoping to speak to Father Tom.'

The young man grinned. 'And so you are.'

This was Father Tom? Zac swallowed his shock. He'd expected a grey-haired old fellow, possibly stooped and wearing spectacles. This Father Tom, with his designer stubble and flashing blue eyes and no hint of a dog collar, looked more like a rock star than a priest.

'How can I help you?' Father Tom asked.

'I'm Zac Corrigan. I—'

'Zac, of course, of course… Wonderful to meet you. Come on in.' The young priest opened the door wider and stepped back. 'Take a seat,' he added as he scooped a pile of hymn books from a chair.

Once the books were deposited on a crammed shelf, he held out his hand. 'Please accept my condolences.' His hand gripped Zac's firmly. 'Liv was an amazing girl, just wonderful. We're all devastated.'

'I'm very grateful that you've offered to fit in a funeral for her at such short notice.'

'Only too happy to help.' Father Tom sat behind his desk, pushed some paperwork aside and leaned forward, hands clasped. 'Is there anything else I can do for you while you're here?'

Zac deliberately tried to relax, with an ankle propped on a knee. 'I know you can't break confidence,' he said carefully. 'But I wondered if Liv ever spoke to you about the baby's father.'

'About his identity?'

'Yes.'

Father Tom shook his head. 'I had no luck there, I'm afraid. Of course, I did raise the question with Liv. I asked her if the father was going to be able to help her or at least support her. She was straight upfront and said that this was *her* baby and she would be the one to care for it. The father was completely out of the scene.'

Zac realised he'd been holding his breath and now he let it out slowly, surprised by an unexpected sense of relief. He wasn't sure how or when it had happened but, some time in the past twenty-four hours, he'd arrived at a point of acceptance and his feelings about the baby had changed. He would be disappointed now if a strange man stepped up to claim her.

'Of course I did talk to Liv about the challenges of being a single mother so far from home,' the priest said. 'I was concerned about her secrecy and I probed to make quite sure that she didn't want the father's help. She assured me that the baby's father hadn't abused her in any way. In fact, she impressed on me that he wasn't a bad guy, but she said she'd put a lot of thought into her future and she knew exactly what she was doing.'

He fixed Zac with a steady gaze. 'She liked to talk about her family and she told me all about you.'

'Her annoying big brother.'

Father Tom gave a smiling shrug.

'She never told me about her pregnancy.'

'Ah, yes, Liv admitted that. She seemed to think she'd given you enough worry over the years. She knew you would have felt compelled to rush over here and to—'

'Interfere,' supplied Zac, tight-lipped.

This brought another sympathetic smile. 'Micro-manage, perhaps.'

Zac nodded. He knew Liv was right. He would have been over here like a shot, bossing her around, trying to order her to come home.

'Liv certainly planned to tell you once the baby was born. She said—I want to show Zac that I can be a brilliant mum and I want him to be finally proud of me.'

Finally? Zac cringed and the back of his neck burned. 'I was already proud of her,' he said gruffly. 'I might have been bossy, but I—I loved her.'

Damn it, he was *not* going to break down again, and certainly not in front of this man.

'I know you loved her,' Father Tom said gently. 'And

I'm sure Liv knew it, too. She was looking forward to showing you her baby. She told me that she couldn't wait to meet you at Heathrow and she fantasised about the moment she handed you your little niece.'

Oh, God. Zac groaned with the effort of holding himself together. Somehow he managed to lurch to his feet and thank Father Tom for his time. They spoke briefly about the service on Monday.

'Thanks for calling in, Zac. I'll see you then.'

They said farewell and Zac was still shaking inside as he strode back through the church to Chloe.

'No leads on the baby's father,' he said tersely and he was infinitely grateful that Chloe didn't press him with further questions as they went outside, where the clouds had parted at last to reveal a glimmer of pale English sunshine.

Chloe knew Zac was tense after his discussion with the clergyman. As the Tube train rushed back into the city, she tried to talk about practical things.

'I don't think we need to buy many more clothes for the baby, unless we see something *really* cute. I've done a little research on the Net and, for now, I think we probably only need formula and bottles and a steriliser, although we should check with the airline to see what they provide for babies on long haul flights.'

'Yeah, and I suppose we'd better ring the hospital and arrange a time to collect Lucy.' Zac looked a little self-conscious as he said the baby's name and Chloe gave him an encouraging smile.

Unfortunately, the look in his eyes when he returned her smile made her stomach drop as if she'd plunged from a great height.

Which was a definite problem. She'd had a few too many of these moments recently. Spending so much time with Zac was taking its toll.

She told herself that it was only natural, that sharing his personal tragedy was bound to have an impact on her own emotions. But now she was beginning to worry about the future. After this time in London, it was going to be so hard to return to their former strictly boss-PA relationship.

It would be hard for her, at least. She would remember all the emotional moments when her feelings for Zac had felt so much deeper and sweeter. Quite possibly, Zac would have no difficulty, though. He was pretty much an expert at keeping his business and personal life in separate compartments.

For Chloe, however, it had become increasingly clear that the sooner she got back to Brisbane and normality, the better. She was thinking about this when she asked, 'Would you like to collect Lucy this afternoon?'

'I don't think so,' Zac answered slowly, as if he was giving the matter careful thought. 'I hope this doesn't sound selfish, but I feel as if I need a little more time to adjust.'

'How much time?' Chloe asked cautiously.

'A decade?'

She must have looked shocked and Zac laughed. 'A joke, Ms Meadows. Don't worry. I'll speak to the hospital about collecting her tomorrow. In the meantime...' His eyes suddenly gleamed with unexpected merriment. 'I think we've earned ourselves a night out, don't you?'

An unhelpful fizzing raced along her veins, as if they were filled with champagne. 'I...I'm not sure,' she said. A night out sounded risky.

Zac frowned at her. 'Surely you don't want to squander this perfect chance to enjoy a Saturday night in London town?'

Even to sensible Chloe it did seem like a wasted opportunity, and she found it especially difficult to voice her very reasonable concerns when her less sensible self was jumping up and down like an excited child.

'Of course you don't,' Zac answered for her. 'We'll have a fabulous night. It's my last night of freedom and it's your duty as my employee to help me enjoy it.'

Before she could summon an effective protest, the train pulled into Oxford Circus and Zac launched to his feet, so the subject was dropped until they'd battled their way out of the crowded Underground and found themselves once more on the footpath.

By then Zac had it all planned and he was quite exuberant. Even though it was at the last minute, he was sure he could wangle a table for two at a good restaurant.

'And what about theatre tickets?' he asked Chloe now, his eyes shining with expectation. 'What sort of show do you feel like seeing? I must admit I could do with a little comedy.'

'Definitely comedy.' Clearly, there was no point in trying to argue about going out with him for the evening. 'We've had enough of real life drama.'

'Great.' Zac was almost boyish in his excitement. 'We'll go shopping this afternoon to buy clothes—for ourselves, not for the baby. We don't have to worry about sticking to carry-on luggage for the journey home. We'll have the suitcase with Lucy's things, anyway, so why not lash out? I'll pay for your new outfit, of course.'

'No,' Chloe said swiftly and firmly.

Zac stopped abruptly and a pedestrian hurrying behind them almost bumped into him. 'Don't be silly, Chloe.' He reached for her hand, but she slipped it into her coat pocket.

'Now you're being stubborn. This night out is my idea.' Zac ignored the pedestrians streaming around them. His attention was solely on Chloe. 'Let me buy you a dress and hang the expense. Think of it as a thank you gift for everything you've—'

'No,' Chloe said again, even more firmly to make sure he got the message. 'Thank you very much, Zac. It's an extremely kind offer, but I can't let you buy me clothes.'

This was one line she knew she mustn't cross. It was the difference between being his PA and a member of his chorus line of girlfriends.

'It's just a dress, Chloe.' Zac's smile was charming now. Bone-meltingly charming.

Chloe could feel her skin warming and her limbs growing languorous. It would be so easy to give in, but she had to remember that this was the special smile Zac used to conquer his countless female victims.

'Chloe, come on, loosen up. You're in London, for heaven's sake. You can't be in London without buying at least one new dress.'

He was right about that, she conceded. She would regret it later if she arrived home without some kind of memento, and what better than a chic new dress from London's famous Oxford Street?

'I was planning to buy a dress anyway,' she said.

Without dropping the smile, Zac narrowed his eyes at her. 'No, you weren't.'

'Of course I was.' She lifted her chin for emphasis and kept her expression deadpan. 'It'll be my Christmas present to myself.'

CHAPTER SIX

BY THE TIME Chloe carried her shopping bags back to her hotel room she felt quite sick. She couldn't believe she'd spent so much money. On one dress.

The expense was almost obscene. She should never have tried the dress on, but as soon as she'd entered the store she'd been seduced, and she hadn't looked at the price tag until it was far too late.

The knee-length dress with cap sleeves had looked so simple and demure on its hanger. Admittedly, it was a bold red and Chloe had never worn such a bright colour before. She usually stuck to soft pinks or browns, but it was Christmas after all, and she was in a mood to be daring. And as soon as she'd stepped into the changing room and slipped the dress on, her senses had instantly fallen under its spell.

The silk lining whispered against her skin like a lover's kiss and when she closed the underarm zip, the dress settled around her like a second skin. Then she'd turned to the mirror and experienced a true *oh-my-God* surprise.

Was that really her?

How could one dress make such a transformation? The bright red seemed to give her complexion a fresh glow and the scooped neckline enhanced the line of her collarbone and décolletage so that she looked... amazing.

As for the fit of the dress, Chloe had no idea how the designer had done it, but he'd managed to give her an hourglass figure. In a blink she'd become positively vain. She couldn't help it. She twisted this way and that, looking at herself from every angle. She'd never dreamed she could look so good and she knew there was no question. She simply *had* to have this dress. She couldn't possibly walk out of the store without it.

It was only after she'd arrived at this decision that she reached for the label and tried to read the price with the help of the mirror. At first she thought she'd made a mistake—she'd read the price upside-down, or back to front or something—so she was still feeling reasonably calm as she took the dress off, once again delighting in the cool slide of the silken lining over her skin.

With the dress back on its hanger, she looked at the price tag again. And almost had a heart attack.

Just as well there was a seat in the changing room or she might have keeled over.

Huddling on the seat in her undies, Chloe wanted to cry. She'd fallen in love with the red dress. While she was wearing it, she'd been quite certain that the designer had dreamed it up just for *her*.

But, dear Lord, the price was horrendous. Normally, she could buy six dresses for that amount and, with the current exchange rate, it would be even worse in Aussie dollars.

A small voice whispered: *That's why this dress looks ten times better on you than any of your old ones.*

And then, in the next breath, Chloe pictured the expression in Zac's eyes when he saw her in this dress, and that was probably about the time her synapses fused and she stopped thinking clearly. She simply got back into her clothes, marched to the counter and handed over her credit card.

Now, as she hung her purchase in the hotel wardrobe, she tried to ignore the sick feeling in the pit of her stomach. She consoled herself that she'd got a bargain with the black platform heels she'd bought to complete the outfit. And she told herself she'd atoned for her sins by buying a beautiful expensive silk scarf for her mother and an equally costly cashmere pullover for her dad.

And now the only sensible thing was to make sure she enjoyed this evening. Surely that couldn't be too hard?

In fact, it was impossible not to enjoy herself. Zac had bought himself a new dark grey suit which he teamed with a fine grey turtleneck instead of a traditional white shirt, which meant that his already devastating good looks now took on an extra sexy European appeal. Chloe found herself staring. And staring some more.

Of course, Zac did quite a bit of staring, too, especially when they arrived at the romantic candlelit restaurant in Piccadilly and Chloe removed her coat.

After he recovered from his initial dropped-jaw shock, he stared at her with an almost bewildered smile, as if he couldn't quite get over the surprise of seeing her all dressed up.

Illogically, Chloe wanted to cry. The look in Zac's eyes was so out of character. So unguarded and intimate...and *unsettling*.

'Ms Meadows, you've outdone yourself,' he murmured and he didn't drag his shimmering gaze from her till the waiter cleared his throat.

'Sir? If you'll come this way, I'll show you to your table...'

'Yes, yes. Thank you.' Zac sent Chloe a wink, as if to cover any embarrassment, and he touched his hand to her elbow ever so lightly to indicate that she should go ahead of him.

To her dismay, his touch set off flashes and sparks and she almost tripped as they wound their way through the tables.

It was a relief to be finally seated but, throughout the meal, Zac's eyes revealed a range of emotions as his initial shock gave way to amused delight, and finally to a more serious smouldering heat that stole Chloe's breath and set her pulses drumming.

Later, she could barely remember the meal although, of course, everything was delicious. She was too absorbed in the experience of being with Zac in such a romantic setting. Everything was so different—their vast distance from Australia, her red dress, the romantic Christmas decorations—and for one night she stopped thinking of herself as his PA. She was a woman very much enjoying the company of an exceptionally handsome and charming man.

Zac was, not surprisingly, an excellent conversationalist, and once they'd been through the typical chat about favourite books and movies, Chloe encouraged him to talk about himself. He told her how, when Liv was three, his family had lived on an island on the Great Barrier Reef for two years while his mother studied, among other things, the nesting habit of sea turtles.

His father couldn't be with them all the time, apparently, because of his work in the central Queensland coalfields, so he used to fly in and out from the island in a seaplane, which also delivered the family's provisions.

To Chloe, who'd only ever lived in the same small house in a Brisbane suburb, this life sounded wonderfully adventurous and romantic. Zac had lived in a timber cottage perched on a hill overlooking the Coral Sea, and from his bedroom he could reach out of the window to pick coconuts. His mother had taught him how to skin dive, and at night she'd built campfires on the beach and, while Liv was curled asleep in her lap, she'd taught Zac all about the stars and planets.

'It's a wonder you didn't become a scientist, too,' Chloe said.

Zac shrugged. 'I started out studying marine science but, after my parents' boat disappeared, I—' A corner of his mouth tilted in a briefly awkward smile. 'I needed to try something completely different.'

'At which you're equally brilliant,' she told him warmly.

His eyes shimmered again as he smiled at her. 'Thank you, Ms Meadows,' he said with exaggerated modesty.

But Chloe was sure that talking about his family couldn't be easy and, as they dug their spoons into a shared dessert of sinfully divine chocolate mousse, she directed the conversation to Lucy. 'Would you like her to have an adventurous childhood like yours?'

'You know, I almost want her life to be boring,' Zac said.

Chloe couldn't help herself. 'That would be such a shame.'

'But boring's safe.'

'It might be safe,' she responded, perhaps a little too vehemently. 'But it's certainly not fun.'

Now Zac regarded her thoughtfully before he helped himself to another spoonful of mousse. 'Sounds to me like you're speaking from experience.'

'I'm afraid I am.'

Of course, he wanted her to explain about this, which was how she ended up telling him about her parents—how her dad had worked in a hardware store and her mum was a teacher's aide, how they'd married late and never expected to have a family, so when baby Chloe arrived at the last moment, she had been a complete and bewildering surprise for them.

'My parents were already very set in their ways, so it was a very quiet life,' she said. 'Mum gave up work to stay at home with me and we didn't have much money, so we didn't go out very much, or entertain, and we only went on holidays every second year. Then it was always to the same place, Maroochydore. I love the beach, of course, but I was too shy to make new friends, so I used to sit under a beach umbrella with my parents and watch the other kids having fun.'

She rolled her eyes. 'I know, I know...that makes me sound like such a loser.'

'A loner, perhaps,' Zac said kindly. 'But hardly a loser.'

'It's not what you'd want for Lucy, though.'

He smiled. 'I guess I'll have to aim for some kind of middle ground.'

A picture flashed into Chloe's thoughts of Zac and Lucy with Marissa Johnson, sharing a new 'middle ground' life together. She found the thought incredibly depressing, so it was probably just as well that they'd reached the bottom of the chocolate mousse and Zac checked his phone for the time.

'We'd better get cracking,' he said. 'Our show's starting soon.'

He took Chloe's hand as they left the restaurant. She knew it was only practical to hold hands as they hurried through the crowds in Piccadilly Circus but, as they passed beneath a dazzling wonderland of Christmas lights, she was excruciatingly conscious of his strong fingers interlinked with hers. She'd almost forgotten the heart-zapping intimacy of even the smallest amount of skin contact.

Then they were in the warmth of the theatre, taking off their coats and settling into comfy velvet-upholstered seats, with all the attendant excitement of the lights being dimmed and the curtain rising...

'My sides are aching from laughing so much,' Chloe said as they stood outside afterwards, waiting for a taxi.

'Mine, too,' said Zac. 'I can't remember the last time I laughed so hard.'

'I'm so glad you picked a comedy.'

'Yeah, laughter's certainly good medicine.'

They were freezing on the footpath, but the air was crystal-clear. Above them stretched a network of lights in the shapes of stars, snowflakes and angels that made the night even more enchanting.

Chloe was still feeling relaxed and happy when they reached their hotel, which was probably why she didn't object when Zac suggested a nightcap in the bar.

'Here, allow me,' he said, stilling her hands with his as she was unbuttoning her coat.

At his touch, she froze, and her heart began thumping as she looked up at him.

The world seemed to stand still and she was trapped by his smiling silver-grey eyes.

'I've been dying to do this all night,' he said softly.

She couldn't breathe as she dropped her gaze to his hands, as she watched his long fingers slowly undo each button, as he gently slipped the coat from her shoulders and let his gaze travel deliberately over her.

'You know this dress is…magnificent.'

Chloe could feel a blush rising from her neck to her cheeks.

'I'm so glad you wouldn't let me pay for it,' Zac said.

'Why is that?'

'You would have chosen something sensible and inexpensive and not nearly as attractive as this.'

Now she couldn't help smiling. Seemed her boss knew her only too well.

'Actually, I have a better idea,' Zac said next as he looked around him at the rather crowded bar. 'Let's not have a drink here. We should go upstairs and get room service.'

And, just like that, alarm bells began clamouring in Chloe's ears—loud and clear—a reality check as effective as the clock at midnight for Cinderella.

There was no way she could share late night drinks in her playboy boss's hotel room. But, before she could insist on staying at the bar, Zac took off for the lift, still carrying her coat. She hurried after him, planning to drag him back, but the lift doors were already opening and there were other guests inside. She didn't want to make a scene so she held her tongue until they reached their floor and were out in the corridor.

'Zac, I don't need a nightcap,' she told him quietly but decisively as they arrived at the door to her room.

He tipped his head to one side with the look a parent might give to a troublesome child. 'You're not going to be a spoilsport.'

Chloe sighed. She should have guessed that this would happen and she should have had a strategy already planned. 'Look, tonight's been wonderful. I've had a fabulous time, but we both need to remember this isn't a date.'

'But it so easily could be.'

This was true and in the confined space of the hallway Chloe could smell Zac's cologne, musky and expensive and very masculine. When she looked up, she saw that his jaw was now lined by an attractive five o'clock shadow.

Help! She was still tingling and zapping from having him take off her coat. Anything more intimate would probably cause her to self-combust.

This was such a dangerous moment. She only had to give the slightest hint of acceptance and Zac Corrigan would be kissing her. And she couldn't pretend that she didn't want to be kissed. It was such a long, long time since she'd been in a man's arms…and this wasn't just any man. It was *Zac!* His lips were so close, so scrumptious, so wonderfully tempting.

The air between them was crackling and sizzling. At any moment, he was going to lean in…

Now she was struggling to remember why this was wrong. *I'll only be another of his Foolish Females.*

'Zac, we can't—'

'Shh.' He touched her arm, sending dizzying warmth

washing over her skin. 'Forget about the office for one night.'

'How can I? How can *you*?'

'Easy,' he said as his thumb rode a sensuous track over her bare arm. 'Tonight you're not my PA and I'm not your boss.'

'But we—'

'Chloe, you're an incredibly sexy woman in a gloriously sexy red dress and I'm the poor, helpless guy who's absolutely smitten by you.'

His words sent shivery heat rushing over her skin. She longed to give in. She was only human after all and Zac was a ridiculously attractive man and she'd been half in love with him for the past three years.

And in the past few days she'd learned so much more to like about him. She'd seen past the handsome façade to the vulnerable boy who'd lost his family and still longed for the safety and security of belonging.

But the yearning that filled her now had little to do with respect or friendship. It was pure and simple lust and all Chloe wanted to do was say yes... She was sinking beneath an overwhelming temptation to close her eyes and lift her face to his.

Why shouldn't she? Just about any girl in her situation would.

What the heck? they'd say. *Why not have some fun for one night? What happens in London stays in London...*

Problem was...while Chloe had been half in love with Zac for all this time, she'd also felt smugly superior to the girls who'd fallen head over heels for him. She'd watched those girls from the sidelines and she knew all too well that one blissful night could so easily lead to weeks and months of regret.

There were so many ways that love could hurt and she'd taken ages to get over Sam's death. She was terrified of risking another version of that heartbreak and pain.

It was so hard to be sensible though. So hard when Zac was a heartbeat away from kissing her... When he was looking at her with a breath-robbing intensity.

'Chloe, has anyone ever told you, you have the most amazing—'

In panic, she pressed a hand to his lips, shutting off the rest of his sentence—which was a pity because she was actually desperate to hear why he thought she was amazing. But it was time to toughen up, time to summon every ounce of her willpower. She lifted her face. 'I have one word for you, Mr Corrigan.'

Zac smiled. 'Please, let it be yes.'

She eyed him sternly. 'Marissa.'

His smile vanished as if the name had landed in his chest like a smart bomb.

'Or, if not Marissa,' Chloe went on, needing to make her message clear, 'substitute the name of whichever girl you decide to marry. *That girl* is where your focus should be.'

She felt terrible though, especially when she heard the shudder of Zac's indrawn breath.

'Good shot, Ms Meadows,' he said softly, and then, with a heavy sigh, he took a step back. From a safer distance, he regarded her with a shakily rueful smile. 'I should have remembered that I can always rely on you to be sensible.'

'That's what you pay me for,' Chloe said crisply and then she turned quickly to open her door. 'As I said, I've had a fabulous evening, so thanks again, Zac, and...and goodnight.'

Without looking back, she stepped inside and closed the door swiftly before she weakened and did something very foolish.

Safely inside, she sagged against the closed door and saw her lovely lamplit room in front of her. *Don't think!*

On the other side of the door Zac was still holding her coat, but it was too bad. She would collect it in the morning. She couldn't see him again now. Not when stupid, stupid tears were streaming down her cheeks.

That was a very close shave.

Zac was scowling as he stared at Chloe's closed door. He'd almost lost his head and broken his own golden rule.

Tonight you're not my PA and I'm not your boss.

How could he have said that?

How could he have been so crass? With Chloe, of all people? His invaluable, irreplaceable Chloe.

He knew she already had zero tolerance when it came to his love life, and now he'd just proven to her that her low opinion was justified.

Damn it. How the hell had his plans to marry someone like Marissa slipped so easily out of his head?

Of course, everything might have followed its proper course tonight if Chloe had stuck to being Chloe. But she'd morphed into a goddess in the sexiest red dress on the planet.

Sure, Zac had always known that Chloe was an attractive young woman, but she'd always been safe as his conservative, efficient PA. Beautiful, yes, but a bit distant and shy. He'd never guessed she had the confidence to dress so glamorously, to reveal herself as a truly sensual, feminine woman.

Tonight's dress had been perfect on her. The rich red had given extra glowing warmth to her complexion, enhancing the lustre of her hair and the dark beauty of her eyes.

And as for the figure-hugging lines and the beguiling scooped neckline…

Zac had been stunned. Transfixed. It was the only explanation he could summon for why he'd stepped over the boss-PA line. For a moment there, he'd allowed himself to acknowledge his secret desire for Chloe. Truth be told, his feelings had felt way deeper than the mere desire he felt for his usual girlfriends.

But Chloe had promptly broken the strange hypnotic spell that gripped him and all it had taken was one word.

In a blink he was thudding back to earth, to his real life, to his new responsibilities, to the way the world would be for him from now on and for ever after.

He supposed he should be grateful to Chloe for reminding him, and for remaining so consistent and sensible. He *was* grateful, or at least he probably would be grateful…eventually…

Now, with a sigh of frustration, Zac unlocked the door to his room and went inside, tossing his and Chloe's coats into an armchair. He let out another sigh as he stood, hands on hips, staring down at the coats as they lay in a pool of lamplight—entangled—with a sleeve of Chloe's coat looped over the shoulder of his coat. Like an embrace.

Mocking him for his foolishness.

It was back to business at breakfast in the hotel dining room next morning. Last night's flirtatious smiles and warm camaraderie were safely relegated to the past.

Chloe was pleased that Zac was cool and serious again—at least she told herself she was pleased, just as she told herself she was relieved that he made no teasing or personal remarks as she started on her melon and yoghurt, while he tucked into his full English breakfast.

Apparently, Zac had even been up early and had already made phone calls to both the airlines and the hospital.

'I've decided that we don't need to buy a car seat while we're here,' he said, getting straight down to business. 'The requirements for fitting them into vehicles are slightly different from country to country. And apparently it's easy enough to get a taxi that's set up for a baby. As for the airlines, they provide bassinets and facilities for heating bottles or whatever.'

Chloe nodded. 'Let's hope Lucy doesn't cry too much during the flight.'

'Indeed,' he agreed gravely.

It was a daunting prospect, flying to the other side of the world with a brand new baby.

Zac frowned. 'Do you think three days will be enough time for us to get used to managing her here before we fly home?'

'Three days? Does that mean you're planning to fly home on Boxing Day?'

'As long as the passport comes through in time. Thank heavens you had the forethought to contact that brilliant agency before we left Brisbane. They've broken all records in fast-tracking Lucy's passport, because of our special circumstances. So do you think Boxing Day will work?'

'It should be fine, I guess.' Chloe was quite sure they shouldn't delay their London stay for a second longer than necessary. And she knew Zac must be eager to get home. He had a great deal to organise when he arrived in Australia—including the procurement of a suitable wife. 'As Lucy's so tiny, she might do a lot of sleeping,' she suggested hopefully.

'Yes, fingers crossed.' Zac handed her a sheet of note-paper. 'I asked the hospital about bottles and formula et cetera. Apparently, we should have collected a checklist, but I've jotted down the things we'll need.'

Chloe scanned the list as she sipped her coffee. Fortunately, she was used to reading Zac's scratchy handwriting. She nodded. 'I noticed there's a pharmacy nearby, so I'll get all these things straight after breakfast.'

'Great.' Zac lifted the coffee pot. 'Like a top-up?'

'Just half a cup, thanks.'

As he concentrated on pouring, he said, 'There is one other difficulty that we haven't discussed.'

'What's that?'

He kept his gaze focused on the coffee pot as he filled his own cup. 'We need to decide where Lucy should sleep.'

'Oh, yes.' This problem had occurred to Chloe, but she'd promptly dismissed it as far too awkward. Now it had to be faced.

Obviously, while they stayed in the hotel, Lucy would be installed in either her room or Zac's. But the big question was—which room was appropriate? Zac was Lucy's official guardian and uncle, but could a bachelor be expected to cope with a newborn baby on his own? Zac had been terrified of simply holding Lucy at the hospital.

'I understand small babies wake at all hours of the night,' he said. 'I read in one of those magazines of yours that newborns sometimes need feeding every two to three hours, even at night time.'

Chloe nodded carefully, certain she could see where this was heading. 'I wouldn't mind taking care of Lucy through the night.'

'No, no,' he said, surprising her. 'I wasn't angling for that. It's asking too much of you.'

'So you think you'll be OK looking after her?'

His mouth squared as he grimaced. 'Frankly, no. I imagine I'll be pretty hopeless.'

'Then, unless you hire a nanny, we don't really have an alternative.'

Zac watched her for a long moment and the smallest hint of a smile played in his eyes. 'Actually, we do have an alternative, Chloe, but I'm afraid you're not going to like it.'

In an instant she was sitting straighter. 'You're not going to suggest we share a room.'

'But it makes sense, doesn't it?' His smile had disappeared now and Chloe could almost believe that he wasn't teasing. 'Neither of us knows much about babies. We both need moral support.'

She groaned. Of course she was remembering last night's close call when Zac had almost kissed her, when she'd almost let him...when she'd so very nearly welcomed him into her arms...and of course the memory stirred all the yearnings that she'd spent an entire night trying to forget. 'Honestly, Zac, don't you ever give up?'

'Calm down. There's no need to get all stirred up and old-maidish.'

'*I am not an old maid,*' Chloe hissed in a rush of righteous fury. Actually, she might have yelled this fact if they weren't in a refined hotel dining room filled with dignified guests.

'I stand corrected.' Straight-faced, Zac pushed his empty plate aside and rested his arms on the table as he leaned towards her. 'I certainly wasn't going to suggest that we share the same bed,' he said, lowering his voice so that she also had to lean in to hear him. 'I've actually looked into hiring a suite with two bedrooms, but the hotel's fully booked with special Christmas deals, so there's nothing like that available. And we really don't want to have to start hunting for another place at this late stage.'

Chloe had to give him credit—there wasn't a trace of a smile or a smirk.

'So what do you have in mind?' She wished her voice didn't sound so shaky.

'Well, it's easy enough to break up a king-size bed into twin singles and then our problem's solved.'

'Solved?' *So we'd be sleeping side by side?* 'What kind of a solution is that?'

'I'm only trying to think of what's best for the baby.' He actually sounded genuine. 'I swear there'll be no funny business, Ms Meadows. I'll be on my best behaviour.'

'I'm sure you have good intentions, Mr Corrigan, but I'd much rather—'

Chloe stopped. She'd been about to say that she would much rather look after Lucy on her own, but then she realised how selfish that sounded, and she would be denying Zac an important chance to get to know his baby niece and possibly to bond with her.

Maybe she *was* being a trifle prudish. After all, if Zac had really wanted to seduce her, he wouldn't have given up so easily last night. And if he could resist her in last night's red dress, he wasn't likely to pounce on her as she walked the floor at midnight with a fretful baby in her arms.

'Look, all right,' she admitted reluctantly. 'I suppose your plan makes a crazy kind of sense. I'll…I'll give it a go.'

Her boss rewarded her with one of his spectacular smiles. 'I knew I could rely on you to be unfailingly sensible. I'll organise for the beds to be changed, and for a cot to be sent up to my room. And I certainly won't let your room go. You'll need it as a bolt-hole, at least to escape to for long hot baths.'

His grey eyes shimmered and she couldn't be sure if he was teasing her again.

CHAPTER SEVEN

'SHE'S AN ABSOLUTE angel, isn't she?'

Zac stood by the cot set in a corner of his hotel room, aware that he wore a sappy smile on his face as he stared down at the sleeping baby. As far as he could tell, Lucy Corrigan was perfect.

She'd been sound asleep when he and Chloe collected her from the hospital and she'd slept all the way during the taxi ride. She hadn't even stirred when they arrived back at the hotel, where he'd rather clumsily extracted her from the car seat before the excited hotel staff rushed to make a huge fuss of them.

Now the three of them were alone. Chloe was in an armchair by the window, reading yet another magazine about mothers and babies, and Zac was pacing the floor on tenterhooks, waiting for Lucy to stir and wake for her next feed.

Standing ready in the bar fridge were a row of bottles of formula that Chloe had made up and which she was going to heat with a special travelling contraption she'd found at the pharmacy.

Zac wasn't entirely happy about this. He'd planned to ask the kitchen staff to prepare the baby's formula and he'd been quite pleased with the idea of Lucy's bottles arriving via room service. He was rather amused by the prospect of signing for a baby's bottle delivered on a covered silver tray.

But Chloe, sensible as always, had wanted to be certain about the hygiene of the bottles and about getting the temperature of the milk exactly right, so now Zac's bathroom housed a sterilising unit as well as the heating gear and a collection of baby bath gels and lotions and wipes.

Still, he liked to think of himself as tolerant—and at least Lucy was very well behaved. Not a peep out of her so far. Then again, a quiet, sleeping baby was rather boring for a guy who wasn't used to sitting around...

'Isn't she due to wake up for a feed?' he asked Chloe as he checked the time yet again. By his reckoning, Lucy had slept twenty minutes past her mealtime.

Chloe looked up from her magazine. 'I suppose she'll wake when she's ready.'

'Isn't that a bit vague? I thought there was a schedule.' Schedules were usually his PA's forte. 'Isn't it important to get a baby into a routine?'

'Zac, give her time. She's only a few days old. She'll probably wake soon.'

Disgruntled, he picked up the TV remote and pressed the 'on' button. A loud blast of music erupted and Lucy gave a start, throwing one tiny arm in the air.

'Sorry,' he muttered as Chloe glared at him while he hastily searched for the 'mute' button.

Ridiculously, his heart was pounding now. No doubt he'd terrified the baby. He held his breath, waiting for her wails of terror. But, to his amazement, she was already asleep again, lying as still as a doll. Perhaps she'd never really woken.

Zac dropped into another armchair and began to flip restlessly through the channels with the sound turned down, but there was nothing he really wanted to watch and he found his mind meandering back over the previous night…

Rather than chastising himself yet again, he allowed himself to dwell on the pleasures of the evening. And there had been many. Chloe had been such good company—so relaxing and easy to talk to at the restaurant—and at the theatre she'd laughed uproariously, even at risqué jokes that he'd feared might upset her.

As for the red dress… Zac feared he was scarred for life by that dress.

He knew that from now on, every time Chloe walked into his office, he was going to remember the tormenting way the dress had hugged her delicious curves.

Why on earth had he paid such scant attention *to* those curves before now? He was beginning to regret that he'd been so disciplined from the day Chloe first joined his staff, never allowing himself to think of her as anything but his PA.

Of course, office romances were messy and bad for business—Zac had seen several of his mates fall by that particular wayside—but, last night, it was as if he'd had laser surgery and his vision had suddenly cleared. And today, even though Chloe had changed back into a sweater and jeans that he'd seen many times before, he was aware of her body in a whole new and entirely distracting way.

He couldn't help noticing the lush swell of her breasts and the dip to her waist, or the sweet tempting curve of her butt.

Which was hardly conducive to a good working relationship, especially now that they were spending so much time together, including sleeping side by side in the same room. Clearly his brain had been out to lunch when he'd come up with *that* bright idea. He'd presumed the baby would keep them fully occupied...

With a heavy sigh, Zac switched off the TV, pushed out of the armchair and began to prowl again. If Lucy slept for too much longer he would have to take off—go for a hike—hope that the freezing winter weather outside might chill his inappropriately lustful thoughts.

'Are you quite sure we shouldn't wake her?' he demanded after yet another circuit of the room.

Chloe rose and came over to the cot. Her sweater had a V-neck that exposed the soft pale skin of her neck and a hint of the perfection of her collarbone.

'I'm not totally sure,' she said. 'Most of the information I've read is for breastfed babies.'

Zac wished she hadn't mentioned breasts. He was all too aware of the way hers swayed gently beneath the soft knit of the sweater when she walked.

He tried to concentrate on the tiny girl as they stood together, looking down at her. Lucy was lying on her side, giving them a view of her profile now—the newborn slope of her brow, her snub little nose and slightly pouting red lips.

She was so still. So quiet. So *tiny.*

A tremor of fear rippled through Zac's innards. 'I suppose she's still breathing?'

He saw his fear reflected in Chloe's dark eyes. 'Of course. Well...I—I think so.'

Zac's fear spiked to panic. 'Should we check?'

'OK.'

One of Lucy's hands was peeking out of the blanket

and his heart hammered as he reached down and touched it with his finger. 'She feels a little cold.'

'Does she?' Chloe also sounded panicked now and she gave the baby a prod with two fingers.

Lucy squirmed and made a snuffling noise.

'Oh, thank God,' Zac breathed and he nearly hugged Chloe with relief.

Then they both laughed, shaking their heads at their foolishness, but, as their smiling gazes connected, Zac's heart thudded for a very different reason.

He felt a deep rush of gratitude for this woman. In the past few days he'd experienced some of the darkest moments of his life and Chloe's presence had been like a gently glowing candle, a shining light just when he needed it. Actually, he suspected that this feeling comprised something way deeper than gratitude.

Perhaps Chloe sensed this, too. Confusion flashed in her eyes and she hastily looked down. 'Hey,' she said suddenly. 'Zac, look.'

From the cot, two small bright eyes were staring up at them.

Zac grinned. 'Well, well…hello there, Lucy Francesca Corrigan. Aren't you the cutest little thing?'

'I guess we can pick her up now,' Chloe said. 'She probably needs changing. Do you want to do the honours?'

Zac swallowed. The nurse had handed the baby to Chloe when they left the hospital, which was fine by him. He'd planned to be an observer. Then again, he'd never been one to chicken out of a challenge.

'OK,' he said bravely, peeling back the top blanket. To reassure himself, he added, 'No worries.' But he held his breath as he carefully lifted the tiny bundle.

'You can change her on the bed,' Chloe said.

'Me?'

'Why not?' Her smiling dark eyes were daring him now. 'I've spread towels for you.'

'Right, sure.'

Anyone would think he was defusing a bomb, the way he gingerly set the baby down and began to unwrap her bunny rug. Beneath this, he found that she was wearing an all-in-one affair, like a spacesuit, so his task now was to undo countless clips.

Beside him, Chloe was on standby with baby wipes and a clean disposable nappy.

'Maybe you should take over,' he suggested. 'You're probably an expert. You've done this before.'

She shook her head. 'I haven't actually, but I've watched friends change babies, and I'd say you're doing a fine job.'

Soldiering on, Zac eventually managed to free Lucy from her nappy and it was a bit of a shock to encounter her naked lower half. Her hips were minuscule, her legs thin and red as she kicked at the air.

'She's like a little frog,' he said in awe.

'She's beautiful,' reproached Chloe.

'Well, yeah. A beautiful little frog.'

Chloe handed him a wipe. 'You can put on a new nappy and dress her again while I heat her bottle.'

'Right.' Zac felt a stab of alarm as Chloe disappeared, but then he took a deep breath and manfully got on with the job and, although it was tricky getting tiny limbs back into the right sections of the garment, he was absurdly pleased with himself when he had Lucy properly dressed again by the time Chloe came back with the bottle.

'She hasn't cried at all,' Chloe commented.

'No, she's frowned and looked cross-eyed at me once or twice,' Zac said. 'But not one wail.'

'Isn't she good?'

'Amazing.' In a burst of magnanimity, he said, 'You can feed her if you like. I'm happy to watch and learn.'

But Zac soon realised this wasn't such a great idea. The picture Chloe made as she settled in the armchair with Lucy made him choke up again. This was partly because he was suddenly thinking of Liv and the fact that she should be here with her baby. But also…even though he was missing Liv, he knew that Chloe looked so damn right in this setting.

Perhaps it was something about the tilt of her head, or the way the light from outside filtered through the hotel's gauzy curtain, making the scene look soft, like a watercolour painting.

Or perhaps it was the fondness in Chloe's face as she looked down at Lucy, and the way Lucy looked straight back at her, concentrating hard, so that she almost went cross-eyed again as she sucked on the teat.

He was damn sure those two were forming a bond.

'I should put the kettle on and make you a cuppa,' he said, wishing his voice didn't sound so gruff.

Chloe flashed him a brilliant smile. 'Thanks.'

As Zac went to fill the kettle he couldn't remember the last time he'd made a cup of tea for anyone else. He knew he should be dismayed by the sudden domestic turn that his life had taken, but the craziest thing was that he actually quite liked it.

Chloe was secretly amazed that the first day with Lucy went so smoothly. After the baby was fed and burped she went straight back to sleep again and she continued to sleep while Chloe and Zac watched an entire DVD.

Now, the short winter daylight had disappeared already and the dark streets outside once again flashed with traffic lights and neon signs and Christmas decorations.

'This baby-raising is a piece of cake,' Zac declared as he poured two glasses of the Italian wine he'd ordered from room service and handed a glass to Chloe. 'How much do they pay babysitters and nannies for sitting around like this?'

'I don't really know,' Chloe said. 'But I'm quite sure they earn it.'

'I can't see how.' Zac was grinning as he lifted the cover on the cheese platter he'd ordered to accompany the wine, and Chloe guessed he wasn't really serious. Then again, it was hard to argue that their new responsibility was onerous as they clinked glasses in a toast to the sleeping baby in the corner.

Their afternoon had been surprisingly pleasant. She and Zac had established clear ground rules and he'd been on his best behaviour…and this evening promised ongoing pleasantness.

They planned to have dinner here in Zac's room and perhaps watch another movie, having discovered an unexpected mutual liking for sci-fi. It was all very agreeable. Zac was so much more at ease about caring for Lucy now and Chloe was genuinely pleased for him. He'd been through so much turmoil over the past few days and he still had to face his sister's funeral in the morning, and heaven knew what challenges awaited him when he got back to Australia.

A quiet, relaxing evening was exactly what he needed

and so they'd planned for dinner at seven-thirty, allowing plenty of time for Lucy to wake and be changed and fed and settled back to sleep again.

Chloe always felt better when she had a clear plan...

'Is that someone knocking?' Zac shot a frowning glance to the door. He couldn't really hear anything with a baby screaming in his ear. 'What's the time?'

'Seven-thirty,' said Chloe, who'd been pacing anxiously beside him.

'That'll be our dinner.' Zac, who was fast becoming an expert, deftly shifted Lucy, plus a hand towel to catch spit-up milk, to his other shoulder. 'We should have rung through and told them to hold the meal till we got her down.'

Chloe winced, knowing that normally she would have thought of this. 'I guess I'd better answer the door.'

'Wait till I take Lucy through to the bathroom. We don't want to blast the poor guy's ears off.'

Chloe's stomach was churning as she watched Zac disappear with the red-faced, yelling babe. This had been going on for over an hour now and they weren't quite sure how or why Lucy was so upset.

She'd woken from her sleep and together they'd bathed her and changed her into clean clothes from head to toe. This had taken a little longer than it probably should have and by the time they'd finished Lucy was desperately hungry and letting them know. When Zac offered her the bottle—they'd decided it was his turn—she had sucked quite greedily and the milk had disappeared in no time.

'Piece of cake, this looking after babies,' he'd said again, smiling smugly as he laid Lucy back in the cot.

Thirty seconds later, the wailing had begun. Lucy kept pulling her little knee into her stomach as if she was in pain.

'She needs burping,' Chloe decided. 'There's a diagram of what you have to do in one of the magazines.' And, following the instructions carefully, she'd sat Lucy on her lap, holding her tummy firmly with one hand while she gently rubbed her back.

It hadn't worked—and neither had walking up and down with Lucy. The hoped-for burp never occurred and after more than an hour of valiant efforts to calm her, her cries still hadn't stopped.

Despite the closed bathroom door, the yells could be heard all too clearly now as their room service dinner was wheeled in...

Chloe gave the fellow a generous tip.

'Thanks.' His eyes were wide with curiosity and he sent more than one worried glance to the closed door.

'Colicky baby,' Chloe told him with the knowledgeable tone she imagined a nursing sister might use. 'She'll settle soon.'

The fellow nodded and hurried away and Chloe hoped they weren't going to be reported for creating a disturbance.

She opened the bathroom door for Zac and he emerged looking somewhat haggard, although Lucy's howls had finally begun to quieten to whimpers.

'Do you think she's settling?'

Zac's shoulders lifted in a shrug. 'I have no idea. From now on I'll admit to total ignorance and I take back everything that I said about nannies and babysitters. Whatever they're paid, it's not enough.'

Chloe couldn't help smiling and, although this wasn't

the right moment, she also couldn't help noticing how utterly enticing a strong hunky man could look with a tiny baby in his arms. Moments like this, she could almost imagine…

But no. She reined her thoughts back. Imaginations were dangerous.

'That dinner smells amazing,' Zac said, casting a longing glance to the trolley.

'I know. My tummy's rumbling.' Zac had ordered a Greek lamb dish for both of them and Chloe doubted any meal could smell more tempting. 'I wonder when we'll get to eat it.'

At that moment, Lucy's knee jerked upwards again and she let out another heart-rending yell.

'She's definitely in pain,' Zac said. 'Maybe we should ring someone. Do you think there's a helpline?'

'I'm pretty sure she just has colic.' Chloe said this more calmly than she felt. 'Early evening is supposed to be the worst time for it.'

'Perhaps it's my fault?' A totally uncharacteristic look of guilt appeared in Zac's eyes. 'Maybe I held the bottle the wrong way.'

'Of course you didn't. Here, let me take her for a bit. You eat your meal. It's getting cold.'

'No, no. You eat first.'

Chloe shook her head. She couldn't possibly eat while Lucy was still so upset. 'Perhaps we should try changing her again…'

In the end, they ate their cooling and congealing dinner in shifts, while taking it in turns to pace the floor with the baby. Several times her crying calmed down and she began to look sleepy and their hopes soared.

Twice she nodded off and they actually placed her back in the cot, holding their breath and hoping she would stay asleep as they backed silently away on tip-toe. Both times, just when they thought all was well, Lucy suddenly threw up her hand and began to cry more lustily than ever.

She kept crying on and off until it was her feed time again. This time, when they changed her, they encountered their first dirty nappy and Zac rose another notch in Chloe's estimation when he didn't flinch, but gamely went to work with the wipes.

He insisted that Chloe be the one to feed Lucy this time. She made sure that the baby didn't guzzle and she stopped the feed halfway through for a little burping session—this time with results—and, to their infinite relief, when they tiptoed away from the cot, Lucy remained sleeping.

As the silence continued, they let out relieved sighs. *Bliss.*

They shared tired smiles.

'I'm knackered,' Zac admitted with a sheepish smile. 'I was looking forward to kicking back with some more of that wine and cheese, but I'm not sure I have the strength.'

'Nor me,' agreed Chloe. 'Not if Lucy's going to wake again in three hours or so.'

She went back to her room to shower and to change into sleepwear and of course she chose the safety of a voluminous grey T-shirt and opaque black tights, but, when she came back, Zac was already in bed and he appeared to be sound asleep.

She smiled wearily. After making such an enormous fuss about the dangers of sleeping so close to Zac, the reality was going to be a non-event. All either of them wanted was the oblivion of deep sleep.

A small sound woke Chloe.

Drowsily, she rolled over without opening her eyes, then nestled back under the covers. No sound now. All was quiet again. Lovely. She didn't have to worry. The sound wasn't Lucy.

Zap!

Lucy? Shocked into wakefulness, Chloe shot up, heart thudding. The room was mostly in darkness, but there was enough light from a lamp in the corner for her to see that Zac was awake and sitting on the edge of his bed.

'I thought I heard something,' she whispered. 'Was it Lucy?'

'It's OK,' he whispered in answer. 'Go back to sleep.'

'But there was a noise. How is she?'

'She's fine. I've just fed her.'

'*You've* fed her?' Chloe stared at him in amazement. 'You mean you've done it all—changed her and fed her and burped her?'

'The whole deal.'

'So what's she doing now?'

'Sleeping again. Like a baby.'

Chloe gave a dazed shake of her head. 'Why didn't you wake me?'

'Didn't want to bother you.' Zac yawned. 'You were snoring your head off.' He yawned again. ''Night. See you in the morning.' And then he lay down with his back to her and pulled the covers high.

Chloe was too surprised to fall straight back to sleep. She was supposed to be moral support. She was sleeping in this room because Zac needed her help. Except he clearly hadn't needed her at all...and she wasn't sure how she felt about that...

She'd grown accustomed to him needing her...

Although perhaps she shouldn't be so surprised. She knew that Zac threw his whole weight into any project he undertook.

As she lay staring into the darkness, she thought again about the fuss she'd made this morning over sharing this room with him. She'd expected him to try to seduce her again. She'd imagined having to fend off his advances, even though she didn't really want to...

If she was brutally honest, she'd probably hoped he might try...

But, as Zac had promised, this was an entirely practical arrangement. He hadn't shown the slightest glimmer of sexual interest in her and now she felt a bit foolish about the way she'd made such a hue and cry.

Of course, it probably helped that she'd chosen to wear these gym clothes to bed rather than slinky pyjamas, but tonight she'd gained the impression that Zac would probably have ignored her even if she'd been wearing a transparent negligee. His focus was entirely on Lucy. And Chloe was delighted about that. She was. Really.

But she wasn't sure if she would get back to sleep.

CHAPTER EIGHT

AFTERWARDS, ZAC'S MEMORIES of Liv's funeral were fragmentary at best. He could recall the harrowing hollowness he felt on entering the small church lit with candles and Christmas brightness, and filled with a surprising number of people. But he remembered very little of the short eulogy he gave, although he did his best to give his sister's new friends a few cheering pictures of Liv's happy family life in Australia, and of the deep love he'd always felt for her.

He thanked everyone gathered there for offering his sister the welcoming warmth of their friendship and for coming today to honour Liv's memory. He thanked Father Tom…having earlier handed him an envelope with a cheque that he hoped would convey his immense gratitude.

Moving outside again was the worst moment—bidding farewell to Liv's coffin before it was driven away. Zac felt as if he couldn't breathe. His throat burned as if he'd swallowed a hot ember and his hand was shaking as he reached into his coat pocket and drew out a piece of coral, one of two pieces he'd found on a shelf in Liv's room.

Bleached white and bony, like miniature antlers, Zac had recognised them immediately as coral their mother had collected when they'd lived on the island, pieces that Liv had always kept with her.

Today he placed one slender branching cluster on her coffin.

'Bye, Liv,' he whispered. Then, blinded by tears, he wrapped his fingers around the other piece still in his pocket.

When he felt an arm slip through his, he turned to see Chloe, who offered him a markedly wobbly smile.

'You were wonderful,' she told him, and her eyes were shiny with tears as she picked up the tail of his scarf and tucked it back inside his coat, before lifting her face to press a warm kiss to his cheek.

Zac closed his eyes, more touched by the simple gesture than was possibly appropriate. He suspected that, while other memories might fade, this particular moment would stay with him for ever.

Even though it was Christmas Eve, Skye and Liv's other housemates insisted on inviting everyone back to the house. In no time the place was crammed with a huge range of young people, including Father Tom.

As mugs of mulled wine and savoury platters were passed around, Chloe was introduced to a fascinating crowd with a wide range of British accents, as well as the more distinctive voices of people who were clearly new arrivals, just as Liv had been.

She met a Brazilian man, a kitchen hand who was not only stunningly handsome but extremely polite and charming. Next, she was introduced to two Polish plumbers with shaved heads who looked fierce but were actually super-friendly. A large West Indian girl showered everyone with her beaming smile.

Of course, all of Liv's friends wanted to make a fuss of Lucy and, to Chloe's surprise, they'd even brought presents for the baby—so many gifts, in fact, that Zac was going to need another suitcase.

Zac was extremely tolerant as the baby was passed around, and Chloe guessed that he was as touched as she was to discover how supportive Liv's community of friends had been. And, fortunately, Lucy seemed to enjoy all the attention.

'That went well,' Zac said quietly as a taxi took them back to the hotel. 'I had no idea what to expect, but it couldn't have been better, really.'

But he still looked sad...terribly sad...and Chloe's heart ached for him.

Almost as soon as they got back to the hotel, Zac made his excuses. 'There are one or two matters I need to see to,' he said enigmatically before disappearing.

Chloe knew he had to collect Lucy's passport, but she was also sure he needed a little time to himself. Actually, she was more than ready for some thinking space, too... There were one or two matters she needed to chew over...including the fact that the longer she was in close proximity to Zac Corrigan the more she liked him, the more she cared about him. Deeply. Maybe even *loved* him...

In the past few days her understanding of her boss had changed massively, especially since they'd begun caring for Lucy. There were times when Zac had looked at her with an emotion that went way deeper than teasing or desire. Moments when Chloe saw a kind of tenderness that made her heart tremble and hold its breath, as if...

Her more sensible self wanted to argue with this, of course, but Chloe was tired of her internal debates...or perhaps she was just plain tired. Lucy had been colicky again in the early hours...

Curled in the armchair, she must have nodded off, and she woke with a start when Zac returned.

'Sorry.' He sent her a smile as he tiptoed across the room to peek into the cot. 'I was trying not to wake you.'

'Doesn't matter. Is Lucy still asleep?'

'Out like a light.'

Chloe's limbs were stiff as she unfurled from her cramped position and sat straighter. She rubbed at her eyes and blinked. No, she hadn't imagined it. Zac was not merely smiling; he was looking particularly pleased with himself.

She'd assumed he'd been walking around London's streets, sunk in his grief, but his smile was definitely triumphant as he tossed his coat onto the end of his bed before he sank comfortably into the other armchair. 'I've collected Lucy's passport and I've sorted out our Christmas,' he said.

'Sorted it how?' Despite the beautiful decorations and lights and the frenzy of shopping all around them, Chloe had almost stopped thinking about Christmas. 'I thought we'd have turkey and plum pudding here in the room.'

'No, Chloe, you deserve better than that.'

'I do?' she asked, frowning.

'Yes, you do, Chloe Meadows.' Zac smiled gently and she wished he wouldn't. 'You've given up your own plans for Christmas without a word of complaint and you deserve some fun.'

An edgy uncertainty launched her to her feet. What was Zac planning? That she should go off and celebrate Christmas on her own while he stayed here with Lucy? She couldn't imagine she'd enjoy that very much.

'Zac, I don't need a fancy Christmas. I've said all along that I'm happy to help with Lucy.'

'Don't worry about Lucy. I've organised a sitter.'

She stared at him in surprise. 'But you don't believe in babysitters.'

Zac frowned. 'I don't think I ever said that exactly.' Now he rose from his chair to stand beside her. 'I'm not keen on nannies, particularly if they're used as a mother substitute. But this is different. It's not fair to you to be locked up in here on Christmas Day with someone else's baby.'

His eyes sparkled. 'After all, I did promise you a flash London Christmas to make up for missing our office party.'

'So you did.' Chloe found that she was smiling too as she remembered what a big deal the office Christmas party had been for her. Only a few days ago. So much had changed since then. And now...the very fact that Zac had obviously been thinking about her, making plans in an effort to please her made her feel unexpectedly happy and glowing...

'Actually, I've also been thinking ahead,' Zac said. 'I've been thinking about when I get home. I've realised that I can't expect *any* woman to be tied to the baby around the clock. She'll have to have help.'

Any woman... He was referring to his future wife, of course, and a shiver skittered down Chloe, as if he'd dropped a cold key down the back of her shirt. How silly she'd been to imagine...to think that he might possibly...

'So,' she said stiffly as she tried to ignore the chilling slap of ridiculous, unwarranted disappointment. 'What do you have planned for tomorrow?'

'Are you all right, Chloe?'

'Yes, of course.' She was working hard now to ignore the confusion and tumult that seemed to have taken up residence in her head and her heart.

Turning away from him to the window, she stared out at the park with its huge bare trees. She saw children in woolly hats chasing each other, saw businessmen with newspapers and furled umbrellas. An elderly couple were walking their dogs. And then her vision blurred.

She certainly wasn't all right. She was very afraid that, against her better judgement, she'd fallen in love with her boss.

She was as foolish as all his other females. More foolish actually, because she'd always known that falling for Zac was dangerous.

Somehow, over the past few days, she'd been seduced by their moments of deep connectedness. She'd been charmed by those times when he'd looked at her with a true appreciation that went way deeper than the mere respect of a boss for a trusted employee.

Saturday night had been different—Chloe had found it difficult but at least possible to resist Zac when he'd so clearly set out to seduce her. After all, she knew that Zac Corrigan would try to seduce any young woman he dated. But this morning, outside the church, Zac had needed her emotional support. And her heart had never felt so full…

'Chloe, what is it? What's the matter?' Zac was standing close behind her now and at any minute he was going to discover her tears.

'I—I was just thinking about...Christmas,' she said, grasping at any excuse.

'I suppose you must be missing your parents.'

'Yes.' Across the street a young woman was running through the park. The woman wore a red coat and her blonde hair was flying behind her like a banner.

'Chloe.' She felt Zac's hand on her shoulder and she tried to keep her head averted. The girl in the park was running to meet a young man. The young man was hurrying too and at any moment they would fall into each other's arms.

'You're crying,' Zac said and he made a soft sound of despair. 'Come here.' With sure hands, he pulled her around to face him. 'Let me see you.'

Chloe shook her head, made her eyes extra wide in a desperate attempt to hold back the tears. *I'm being an idiot.*

Zac had positioned her in front of him now, a hand on each of her shoulders as he searched her face, his grey eyes mirrors of her sadness. 'Chloe, what's the matter?'

How could she tell him? She shook her head and she might have held up her hand to ward him off but, before she could, his arms were around her, drawing her against him.

'Oh, Chloe.'

Now she was clinging to him, pressing her damp face into the comforting wall of his chest, and his arms were around her, warm and strong, holding her close. She could smell a faint trace of his aftershave, could hear his ragged breathing, could feel his heart thudding against hers. Now she could feel his lips brushing a soft kiss to her brow...and that tiny intimacy was all it took.

In the next breath she was coming undone, wanted nothing more than for Zac to kiss her properly. On the lips. And if he kissed her, she would kiss him back. She would kiss him deeply, passionately, throw caution to the wind.

With him suddenly so close, her emotions were a fiercely rushing tide. Desire churned deep inside her, and she knew she had no choice but to ride the flood... rising, rising... She was gripped by a kind of desperation. It was now or never... If Zac kissed her, she would surrender. She would give herself to him completely. Nothing else mattered.

Oh, how she longed for him to kiss her.

Fortunately, he was a mind reader.

With a hand beneath her chin, he lifted her face and touched his lips to hers and everything went wild. Their kiss flared from hello to explosive in a heartbeat and Chloe wound her arms around his neck, pressing close, turning to fire.

Neither of them spoke. It was as if they both feared that words might break the spell. This coming together was all about emotion and longing and heat...as their mouths hungered and their hands turned feverish...as clothing fell silently onto white carpet...as they stumbled in a lip-locked tango to the nearest bed.

For a fleeting second, as they landed together on the mattress, Chloe's more sensible self tried to slam on the brakes. But Zac was gazing down at her and he had that look in his eyes—a look that was a mix of heartbreak and surprise and unmistakable desire. A look that melted her.

And now his hand was gliding over her skin and

flames leapt to life wherever he touched. He lowered his lips to her breast and the longing inside Chloe bucked like a wild beast fighting to be free. All hope of resistance was lost…

Afterwards…the thrashing of their heartbeats gradually subsided as they lay side by side… And the silence continued…

Chloe couldn't find the right words. What did you say to your boss when you'd just shared blazing, uninhibited, mind-blowing sex with him? She had no idea, and it seemed Zac had been struck dumb as well.

Cautiously, she turned her face towards him. With equal caution, he turned to her and his eyes reflected the same shell-shock she felt.

They both knew this wasn't supposed to happen. They'd clarified on Saturday night that there were very valid reasons why this should never happen.

But now…their lovemaking had been so spontaneous, so flaming and passionate, it had taken them both by storm.

'Are—are you OK?' Zac asked gently, his words touching her skin and reaching into her heart, just as his kisses had, mere moments ago.

'Yes,' Chloe whispered.

He let out a huff of breath and a soft sound that might have been a sigh or the merest hint of a laugh. 'At least one of us is OK then.'

What did he mean? She knew she should ask, should at least say *something,* but she certainly wasn't willing to analyse the whys and wherefores of this, and she was still struggling to find the right words when Lucy woke with a lusty yell.

Grateful for the distraction, both Chloe and Zac rolled out of opposite sides of the bed and began to drag on clothes with the speed of commandos responding to an alarm.

'You can heat the formula,' Chloe said as she pulled her shirt over her head. Zac knew how to look after the formula now and he was quite expert at testing the temperature of the milk on the inside of his wrist. He was standing by with Lucy's bottle when Chloe had changed her nappy and re-dressed her.

'Why don't you feed her?' Chloe suggested, without quite meeting his gaze. 'I'll make a cup of tea.' OK, so perhaps it was another ploy to avoid talking to him about what had just happened, but the tea making had also become part of their surprisingly domesticated routine. 'Then you can tell me what you have planned for Christmas,' she added.

'Christmas?' Zac gave a soft, self-deprecating laugh. 'Went clear out of my mind.'

'And remember, don't let her guzzle,' Chloe warned, desperately needing to remain businesslike and matter-of-fact, but her thoughts were churning as she went to fill the kettle.

Zac found it hard to concentrate on feeding the baby. He had too much to think about. He'd always believed he was reasonably knowledgeable when it came to women and seduction. He'd also thought he knew his PA quite well. He'd been wrong on both counts and to say that he was stunned was putting it mildly.

He cringed now when he recalled accusing Chloe of being an old maid. Clearly, she was far more worldly than he'd ever dreamed. He didn't want to start mak-

ing comparisons, but something amazingly spontaneous and earth-shatteringly good had happened just now.
Something way, *way* beyond random meaningless sex…

No doubt he'd stuffed up the very fine working relationship he had with his PA, however, and that was damn
stupid. At this point, he had no idea where to take things
from here, but one thing was certain—he would have
to think this situation through very carefully before he
made another move.

Perhaps his Christmas plans would be a useful diver-
sion. He'd pulled off quite a coup, managing to wangle
tickets for the hotel's sumptuous Christmas banquet.
There was to be a six-course menu with every delicacy
imaginable.

He reckoned the best news was that he'd secured a
properly certified babysitter for the entire afternoon. Of
course, he'd had to pay an exorbitant sum for a sitter on
Christmas Day and at such late notice but, with the help
of the concierge, it was all settled.

He'd been really looking forward to sharing this news
with Chloe, but now…a Christmas feast paled into in-
significance after what they'd just shared.

As Chloe poured boiling water over tea bags, her mind
was spinning. Why hadn't she remembered that leaping
into bed with Zac was simply *not* an option? Clearly her
brain had snapped. She'd fallen into the oldest trap—
giving in to lust and confusing it with love.

Surely she knew better than that? She was opening
herself up to all kinds of pain.

Zac was never going to love her, so the outcome could
only be painful. After all, she'd experienced what it was
like to truly love someone and to be loved in return. And

she knew Zac's attitude to love was light years away from her own. He was focused on finding a wife from a database, rather than searching his heart.

Her problem was that she'd spent too much time in his company. She'd become too caught up in his personal life and, for a short time, she'd totally lost her perspective.

Her only choice now was to accept that she'd made a very silly mistake and then to forgive herself. Forgive and forget. That was what Zac would expect her to do and, with luck, she would survive the emotional fallout.

OK. She felt marginally better now that she'd thought this through. It meant she simply had to put her feelings for her boss on ice until she got back to Australia and then she should be safe. She would come to her senses. Surely that was a workable plan?

Their lunch of toasted ham, cheese and tomato sandwiches with coffee was a strained and quiet affair.

'I guess we should talk about…you know,' Zac said as he finished his second sandwich, but he still looked extremely uncomfortable.

Chloe drew a quick breath for courage. 'If you like… but I don't expect a post-mortem.'

'What about an apology?'

Shyly, she shook her head. They both knew this had been a two-sided affair.

'That's good,' Zac said. 'Because I wouldn't want to apologise for something so—'

He left the sentence unfinished, as if words were inadequate…or too revealing…

'Maybe it was inevitable,' Chloe said without looking at him. 'A guy and a girl in constant close proximity.'

When she looked up, she saw his puzzled smile. No doubt he'd expected tears and recrimination. That would have to wait till later when she was alone.

'Chloe, for the record, I'd like you to know that—' Zac hesitated again and his throat worked. 'It's so hard to express this properly, but you must know that kind of chemistry is pretty damn rare.'

Heat flooded her face. For her, their lovemaking had been astonishing, an outpouring of passion beyond anything she'd ever experienced—even with Sam—but she mustn't think about what that signified, or she'd end up with a broken heart. 'Maybe it's best if we don't say too much right now,' she said.

Zac nodded, a cautious smile still playing at the corner of his mouth as he picked up a final sandwich. 'A cooling-off period.'

'Yes.' She was too worried that she'd let her emotions show, that she'd burst into tears and make an awkward situation a thousand times worse.

'I'm sure that's probably wise,' Zac said, but he looked thoughtful, as if he was in the middle of a puzzle he hadn't quite solved. Then his expression lightened. 'Actually, to change the subject, I was wondering if we should brave the elements this afternoon and take Lucy for a walk.'

It was a brilliant idea. Chloe nodded enthusiastically. 'I think we're all in need of fresh air. If we put a little bonnet and mittens on her and bundle her in an extra warm blanket, she should be fine.'

Seemed they were both eager to hit the streets for a final Christmas shopping spree, and Chloe hoped fervently that the bustle of crowds and the dazzle of decorations would prove a very welcome distraction from her way too sexy employer.

'I'm keen to buy something for Lucy's first Christmas,' Zac said as they headed down Oxford Street. 'Any ideas?'

'I was thinking this morning, when Skye was madly taking photos, that it would be lovely to start an album for Lucy and to include shots of London.'

'Good thinking.' He didn't add *Ms Meadows* this time, but he was smiling again, almost back to the Zac of old. 'Lucy should have a record that begins right here with her very first Christmas.'

'I took photos of Skye and her friends with my phone. I'll email them to you, if you like.'

'Great. They should certainly be part of the record.' He definitely looked pleased. 'So an album's first on our list. What else? Liv already bought Lucy her first teddy bear.'

'Maybe you could buy her a gorgeous Christmas stocking while you're here, something that will become a tradition for her every year.'

'Yep, sounds good.' Zac trapped her with a private smile. 'Am I right in guessing you're a girl who likes traditions?'

'Possibly.'

For too long, they stood in the crowded and busy store, smiling goofily at each other until they realised they were blocking an aisle.

'And I think I'd like Lucy to have a little gold bracelet,' Zac said. 'I remember Liv used to wear one when she was a kid.'

'With a heart locket?' Chloe asked.

'Yes.'

She smiled. 'I had one of those too. I loved it, but I lost it once when my neighbours took me water-skiing.'

Zac's grey eyes shimmered and Chloe gulped. She was so susceptible to that look. 'What's the matter? Do I have a smut on my face?'

'I'm trying to picture you as a little girl.'

Her heart tumbled like a snowball on a very steep slope. 'Don't talk like that,' she said, almost begging him. 'Concentrate on the shopping.'

CHAPTER NINE

AT BREAKFAST ON Christmas morning, when Chloe announced that she would like to go to church, Zac surprised her by saying that he'd like to come too.

'Church two days in a row?' she queried.

'I've been reading about St Paul's Cathedral.' Apparently, Zac was fascinated by the cathedral's history. It was rebuilt after the Great Fire of London in 1666, and then later survived the Blitz in World War II when most of the surrounding buildings were flattened in bombing raids. 'It's become a symbol of resurrection and rebirth,' Zac said. 'And that seems rather fitting for Lucy's first Christmas.'

Considering the sad and miraculous circumstances of Lucy's birth such a few short days ago, Chloe had to agree.

'I don't think another outing will hurt her, do you?' he asked.

'She should be fine. She was actually better last night after all that shopping.'

While Zac checked the times of the services, Chloe rang her parents, who had almost finished their Christmas Day in Australia.

'It was wonderful,' they gushed. 'The loveliest Christmas, Chloe. The chauffeur took us to church and then brought us back here in time for lunch. And, my goodness, you should have seen the spread. We've never eaten so well. Please give our love to Zac.'

'My parents are probably your biggest fans,' she told Zac as she hung up, and she felt unexpectedly happy at the thought of going off with him and Lucy to celebrate Christmas in St Paul's.

OK, it might feel like the three of you are almost a proper family, but don't get ideas, girl.

'We've time for presents before we go,' Zac announced as they finished their simple breakfast of coffee and croissants, in lieu of the banquet to come. With a boyish grin, he crossed to the wardrobe and produced a small package.

'Hang on.' Chloe dived for the floor and rummaged under her bed. 'I have a little something for you, too.'

It was also a small gift, but the shop assistant had worked magic with a square of green and white striped paper and a bright red bow. Chloe set the gift on the table in front of Zac, rather than placing it in his hand. Probably an over-the-top precaution, but after yesterday's 'mistake', she was super-conscious of the dangers of any skin contact with this man.

Zac, however, had no qualms about kissing her cheek as he handed her his gift. 'Merry Christmas, Chloe,' he said warmly.

'Thank you.' She knew she couldn't refuse to return his kiss, but she did this so quickly she barely touched his cheek. 'And Merry Christmas to you.' She nodded towards the little green and white package.

'Thanks!' He looked so genuinely delighted that she

wondered how he normally spent his Christmases. It was possible that, without close family, he was often quite lonely. The thought stabbed at her soft heart.

'Aren't you going to open it?' Zac had already freed the red ribbon and had started ripping into the paper.

'Yes, of course.' Her parcel was wrapped in pink and silver tissue and topped by a posy of tiny silk roses. 'But it's almost too pretty to open.'

Zac grinned. 'Go on, get stuck into it. I dare you.'

Chloe laughed. She was actually far more excited than she should have been, but a hand-selected gift from Zac was quite a novelty. Back in Brisbane, it was her job to order his corporate gifts for employees and business associates, as well as sending flowers and perfume to his girlfriends.

His gift to her usually came in the form of a Christmas bonus and, generous and welcome as this was, she couldn't help being curious about what he might buy when he made the selection entirely on his own.

There was a box inside the wrapping and it looked like a jewellery box. Chloe's heart fluttered and she shot a quick glance to see if Zac had opened his gift.

He was watching her and smiling. 'You go first.'

'All right.' She knew her cheeks were pink as she lifted the lid to find, nestling inside in a bed of cream silk, a solid gold chain bracelet with a heart-shaped locket. 'Oh, Zac, it's beautiful. It's just like Lucy's.'

'Hopefully, a grown-up version.'

'Yes, a *very* grown-up version.' Unlike the delicacy of the baby's bracelet, this one was solid and shiny gold and Chloe knew it had probably cost a small fortune.

'I almost bought you a necklace,' Zac said, 'but I

knew you'd lost your bracelet when you were little.' He gave a self-conscious little smile and shrugged. 'I thought you might like a replacement.'

This was so much more than a replacement. It was a gift that mirrored the one Zac had bought for his niece. It wasn't only expensive, it was *personal*...

There was a good chance Chloe's blush deepened. 'I'll love wearing this. Thank you.' On her wrist it looked perfect. Toning beautifully with her skin, it made her feel mega glamorous.

She looked pointedly at the box in Zac's hand. 'Your turn.'

'Ah, yes...'

Chloe held her breath as he lifted the lid on the silver cufflinks she'd bought him. She watched his face, saw the flash in his grey eyes when he recognised the significance, and his face broke into a delighted grin. 'Sea turtles!' His grin broadened. 'You remembered from the other night.'

'I loved your story about living on the island and I thought these were incredibly stylish but cute,' Chloe said. 'But I also thought they might bring back happy memories.'

'They do. They will. They're wonderful.' He looked as if he might have hugged her, but perhaps he'd picked up on her caution. Perhaps he was as afraid as she was that they'd end up in bed again, ravishing each other...

'Thank you, Chloe,' he said instead, but his eyes had that look again, the one that told her he was remembering every detail of their passion, the look that made her head spin and her insides tremble.

* * *

'I feel dangerously virtuous after all that carol singing.'
Zac was in high spirits as they came back into the hotel
room. 'I'm certainly ready to eat, drink and be merry.'

Chloe knew what he meant. She'd felt wonderfully
uplifted by the beautiful music in the magnificent cathedral and it seemed somehow perfect to follow up
with her first slap-up Christmas dinner in a posh hotel.

Just the same, Zac's flippant comment about dangerous virtue sent her thoughts off once again in inappropriate directions, which was probably why she made herself
busy writing notes for the babysitter, double-checking
with room service for the delivery of the sitter's special
Christmas dinner, and ensuring that everything Lucy
might need was already laid out for her.

'At least we'll only be a few floors away, so the sitter
can call us if she has any worries.'

Zac pulled a face. 'I wouldn't encourage her to call.'

'But we have to leave her a phone number, Zac.'

'Oh, if you insist.' His smile was teasing again as he
walked to the cot. 'You go and get ready, while I have
a quiet talk to this child. It's time I delivered her first
lecture. She needs to understand that we expect nothing
from her but her very best behaviour.'

For Chloe, entering the hotel's special banquet room
was like walking into the dining room of a royal palace.
There was so much to take in—the high ornate ceiling
and stunning red walls with huge mirrors that reflected
back the splendour, a tall Christmas tree covered in fairy
lights in the corner, candles everywhere in glass hold-
ers, chandeliers overhead.

Down the middle of the room stretched long tables covered in red tartan and set with sparkling glassware, shining silver, starched white napkins. The guests were beautifully dressed and Chloe was more pleased than ever that she'd lashed out on her expensive red number.

With a glass of Yuletide punch in her hand, Zac's lovely bracelet on her wrist and his tall, dark and exceptionally handsome presence at her side, she'd never felt more glamorous and confident.

She had such a good time. They met a lovely Canadian couple who'd come to England to track down their family history, two genial elderly Scottish brothers who apparently spent Christmas at this hotel every year, a group of New Zealanders…

There was even a famous American author called Gloria Hart, who was accompanied by a much younger man whom she openly introduced as her lover. Chloe had read a few of her books, so meeting her was quite a fan girl moment.

Gloria made a beeline for Zac and although she kept her arm firmly linked with her young man's, she made sheep's eyes at him, and then she turned to Chloe with a coy smile. 'I do like your young man,' she said. 'I'm almost jealous.'

'Ah, but I'm taken,' Zac said gallantly as he slipped his arm around Chloe's shoulders and dropped a proprietorial kiss on her cheek.

Chloe hoped her smile held. Zac probably had no idea that his simple gesture gave her lightning bolts of both pleasure and pain.

Champagne was opened as they all took their seats and settled in for a truly sensational meal. White-coated waiters brought the most amazing dishes—Colchester rock oysters, shellfish platters, roast middle white pork with winter jelly, roast goose with Brussels sprouts and all the trimmings. These were followed by mince pies, Christmas pudding, Ayrshire cream and cider and chestnut syllabub.

Fortunately, there was plenty of time between courses, plenty of laughter and storytelling. Zac, as always, drew more than his share of feminine interest, but he got on well with the men, too, and he was attentive to Chloe throughout the afternoon.

Like Gloria Hart, everyone assumed they were a couple. Chloe almost set them straight, but then she caught Zac's eye and saw an ever so subtle warning smile, as if he was urging her to leave things be. She could almost hear him say, *What's the harm in a little pretence?*

She just wished she could feel happier about it, wished she didn't mind that it was only a charade...

Of course, when she explained that the occasional texts she sent were to their sitter, it was also assumed that she and Zac were Lucy's parents.

'You've regained your figure so quickly,' one woman commented.

Chloe smiled her thanks and this time she avoided catching Zac's eye. But she couldn't help silly thoughts that began with the fireworks of yesterday's unforgettable passion and ended with the bleak sadness of *if only...*

Give up now, Chloe. You know it's never going to happen...and you're not in love with him. You can't be. She didn't want to fall in love again, couldn't bear to risk that kind of heartbreak. And falling for Zac could bring nothing but heartbreak. She knew him too well. *Just play the game. It's only for a few more hours and tomorrow you'll be on the plane, safely winging your way home.*

In the breaks between courses, people got up and moved about, mingling and chatting with other guests, going to the tall windows at the far end of the room to look out at the views across the park. Twice, Zac went back to the room to check on Lucy, which made Chloe smile.

The second time he left was just before their coffee arrived, and when he came back he hurried to Chloe and leaned close to her ear. 'Come with me,' he whispered.

Turning, she saw unmistakable excitement in his eyes and he nodded to the windows. 'I want to show you something.'

'What is it?'

His smile was the sort that made her ache inside. 'Come and see for yourself.'

Of course she was curious, so she excused herself from her neighbour and Zac grabbed her hand, hurrying her to the far end of the room.

'Look.'

Chloe looked and gasped.

Outside, it was dark, but the street lights and the lights of the buildings caught the dazzle of dancing, snowy white flakes. *Snow!* Real, no-doubt-about-it snow was falling silently, landing on tree branches, along railings and on the roofs of parked cars.

'Wow!' she exclaimed, gripping Zac's hand in her excitement. 'I've never seen snow before. Isn't it beautiful?'

'I thought you'd like it.'

'Oh, Zac, it's amazing. It's the perfect end to a perfect day.'

'I don't know how long it will last. I vote we skip coffee and go outside to dance about in it.'

'Yes, I'd love to. But we'll need to go back for our coats and gloves.'

'All sorted. I collected them while I was up check-ing on Lucy.'

Lucy. 'I forgot to ask. How is she?'

'She's fine, Chloe. The lecture I gave her paid off. She's a fast learner.' Zac slipped his arm through hers and gave a tug. 'Come on. Let's go.'

They made their farewells.

'It's snowing,' Chloe explained, which caused quite a stir. 'I'm afraid I've never seen snow before, so we're going outside. I want to catch the full experience.'

'Yes, off you go, lass,' one of the Scotsmen said. 'Al-though I should warn you that London doesn't have real snow.'

'Zac, make sure you keep Chloe warm,' called Glo-ria Hart.

They were laughing as they left amidst calls of 'Goodbye, lovely to meet you' and 'Merry Christmas'.

Chloe hadn't thought it was possible for her Christmas Day to get any better, but she was floating with happi-ness as Zac slipped his arm around her shoulders and they walked together along the paths in the park while the snow fell softly all around them.

'I'm going to wake up soon,' she said, holding out a red-gloved hand to catch a flurry of snowflakes. 'This is so magical. It's simply too good to be true.'

'It might not stay pretty, so I wanted you to enjoy it while it's fresh.'

She looked back to the hotel, where she could see the big window of the dining room, the twinkling lights of the Christmas tree and the chandeliers, and the silhou-ettes of people moving about inside.

'Thanks for dragging yourself away from the party

and bringing me out here,' she said. 'I would have hated to miss this.'

'So would I,' Zac said with a mysterious shy smile.

Even though it was dark now, the park was well lit and the space rang with the excited shouts and laughter of children and adults alike, making the most of the white Christmas. Chloe was zinging with excitement as she and Zac walked on, under bare-branched trees that now gathered white coats, and she loved the way he kept his arm securely around her...

They reached the far side of the park and were turning back when Zac said, 'Actually, while I'm in your good books, Chloe, I wonder if I could put a proposal to you.'

She frowned at this. Something about Zac's careful tone took the high gloss off her happiness. Thinking fast, she tried to guess what this proposal might be about. No doubt something to do with work, or with Lucy, or possibly with Marissa Johnson. She certainly hoped it wasn't Marissa. Not now. Not today.

'What kind of proposal?' she asked cautiously.

'Actually, I was thinking of a marriage proposal.'

Chloe's reaction was inevitable. Her silly heart toppled and crashed.

'Your proposal to Marissa?' She knew her shoulders drooped. She thought Zac had more tact than to bring this up now and spoil Christmas Day.

He gave a soft groan and came to a standstill. 'No, Chloe. This has nothing to do with Marissa.' He was standing in front of her now, blocking her path, as white flecks of snow floated onto his shiny black hair. 'I want to ask you to marry me.'

Chloe struggled to breathe as she stared at him and a cyclone of emotions whirled chaotically inside her, stirring all the longing she'd ever felt for him, along with the confusion and pain, the sympathy and tenderness.

For a giddy moment she allowed herself to picture being married to Zac and of course her silly brain zapped straight back to yesterday's lovemaking and she was instantly melting at the thought of a lifetime of fabulous sex.

And she thought about Lucy. The baby was now an inevitable part of the Zac Corrigan package, and Chloe knew she would adore taking care of the little girl and stepping into the role as her mother. And then there was Zac's business which Chloe knew inside out and was almost as passionate about as he was.

For so many reasons his proposal felt right. But, oh, dear heavens, she had to be careful. She had to remember that this gorgeous, kind and generous man was also the playboy she knew all too well. As far as she could tell, Zac had no real concept of being faithful. As for love… for crying out loud, until five minutes ago, he was planning to pick his prospective wife from a spreadsheet.

Chloe shivered inside her warm coat. 'Don't play games,' she said wearily. 'Not today, Zac. Please, don't be silly.'

He gave an angry shake of his head. 'Why do you always assume I'm playing games? I'm absolutely serious. Think about it, Chloe. It makes so much sense.'

'Sense?' Her eyes stung and it wasn't from the cold. 'I thought you liked to be sensible.'

Oh, give me a break, Zac. How many girls want to be sensible about romance?

But the question wasn't worth voicing. 'So why is this so sensible?' she demanded instead. 'Because I tick most of the boxes on your checklist?'

Zac looked surprised. '*Most* of the boxes? Chloe, you tick every single one of them. Actually, I'd have to add extra boxes for you. You're an amazing girl.'

'And I'm so good with Lucy,' she added flatly.

His smile wavered. 'Well, yes,' he said as if this was obvious.

Oh, Lord. Chloe couldn't hold back a heavy, shuddering sigh. *Please, please, don't let me cry.*

Zac stood very still now, watching her with troubled eyes. He wasn't wearing his scarf and she could see the movement of his throat as he swallowed uncomfortably. 'I've stuffed this up, haven't I?' he said quietly.

Fighting tears, Chloe gave a helpless flap of her hands. 'Maybe you got carried away after the luncheon today, when everyone assumed we were married.'

Now, with his hands plunged into his coat pockets, he tipped his head back and stared up at the dark sky. He sighed, releasing his breath in a soft white cloud. 'Give me some credit, Chloe.'

She could feel the weight of the gold bracelet around her wrist, reminding her of their happiness this morning when they went to church together and opened their presents. She hated that this had happened, hated that they were so tense now, on the raw edge of a fight, at the end of this beautiful, perfect day.

'Can I ask you a difficult question, Zac?'

He looked doubtful, but he nodded.

'Are you honestly in love with me?'

'Honestly?' he repeated, looking more worried than ever.

'There's no point in lying,' she said bravely. 'I know we've been pretending to others all day, but I need brutal honesty now.'

There was a long uncomfortable silence as Zac stood staring at her, his silver-grey eyes betraying a haunted uncertainty. He seemed to try for a smile and miss, then he said, 'I told you I don't really believe in "love".' He made air quotes around the word. 'And I'm afraid that's the truth. I think it's a dangerous illusion.'

Lifting his hands, palms up, as if protesting his innocence, he smiled. 'But I really like you, Chloe. As I said before, I think you're amazing. And you can't deny we have fabulous chemistry.'

A sad little laugh escaped her. Here she was in the perfect romantic setting for a marriage proposal, and instead she received a sensible, practical, *logical* proposal without a glimmer of romance.

Zac's eyes were shiny as he watched her. 'So…I take it that's a no then?'

Oh, Zac.

She had an eerie sense of time standing still. She felt so torn. She knew this was her big chance to be reckless and brave and to grab a wonderful opportunity. She had no doubt she could give her heart to Zac and to Lucy, along with her loyalty to ZedCee Management Consultants.

But the big question was—what could she expect from Zac in return? A comfortable, entertaining, possibly exciting lifestyle…until his interest in her waned.

She was far too familiar with the pattern of Zac's love life. When it came to women, he had the attention span of a two-year-old, and if Chloe was ever going to risk love again, she needed certainty. She needed a man who could bring himself to say and mean those dreaded words: *I love you.*

'I'm sorry,' she said, fighting tears. 'I'm still an idealist. A romantic, I guess.'

'So you want an admission of true love *as well as* brutal honesty? *And* you want both from the same man?' Zac shook his head and it was clear he believed she was asking for the impossible.

Inevitably, the day ended on a low note.

There was no reassuring arm around Chloe's shoulders as they went back to the hotel, where they shook out their snowy coats and took the lift upstairs to find Lucy fast asleep and the sitter about to watch the Queen's Christmas message on TV.

So they watched the royal message with the sitter and then she left them with some reluctance, assuring them that she'd had a lovely day.

And Chloe left, too, going next door to remove her make-up and to change out of her red dress. She put the bracelet back in its box, and stowed it in her already packed suitcase. Then she added the dress, carefully folded between sheets of tissue paper.

Although she wanted to cry, she forced herself to be strong as she cleaned her teeth, creamed her face and brushed her hair.

A faint *'waa...'* from next door warned her that Lucy was awake so, although she really didn't want to face Zac again this evening, she went back to his room to help with the evening feed, which was often the most difficult and colicky time.

However, the baby settled quickly, even before Zac and Chloe had drunk their ritual cuppas, but Chloe didn't join Zac in the armchairs for a cosy chat.

'I'll get on with Lucy's packing,' she said, knowing

they would need to head for Heathrow soon after breakfast in the morning.

Taking up space in the middle of the room, Zac managed to look spectacularly manly and helpless. 'Anything
I can do to help?'

'Probably better if I look after it,' Chloe muttered,
ducking around him. 'I have a list.'

He smiled crookedly. 'Of course you do.'

She was so anxious and edgy and sad, she was glad
of an excuse to keep busy, collecting scattered items like
a baby sock from behind a cushion, a bib from beneath
a pillow, and sorting out exactly what they'd need for
Lucy on the journey. She packed a special carry-on bag
with baby bottles, formula, nappies, wipes and several
changes of clothes. Then she double-checked all their
passports and travel documents.

'I've already checked those papers,' Zac said.

'Doesn't hurt to check again.'

Now that she'd rejected his marriage proposal and
their final evening was ruined, she was extra keen to
be on her way. If there was a hitch at the airport tomorrow—anything that meant they couldn't leave the UK—
she was likely to have some kind of breakdown.

She wanted to be home. She needed to be caring for
her boring sweet parents, needed to get her life back
to normal as quickly as possible. Once she was safely
home, she would put this London experience and everything that came with it behind her. Once again she would
be nothing more than Zac Corrigan's highly efficient and
more or less invisible PA. As always, she would co-ordi-
nate his private life as well as his business affairs, while
she secretly turned up her nose at his *Foolish Females*.

CHAPTER TEN

ZAC WAS BEGINNING to suspect that Lucy could pick up on their vibes. Tonight he and Chloe were both as tense as tripwires, and Lucy was fussier than ever after her next feed. It was close to midnight before she settled back to sleep.

'We're going to have a hell of a trip home if she's like this tomorrow night,' Chloe commented tiredly.

'It will help if we make sure we're relaxed.'

'Relaxed?' The word snapped from Chloe like a rifle shot and, out of the corner of his eye, Zac saw the baby flinch.

He sighed. 'Look, I apologise if I've spoiled your Christmas. I know I've upset you.'

'Of course you haven't upset me. I'm fine.' Chloe's eyes were unnaturally wide as she said this and she promptly made an about-turn and headed for the door.

'Where are you going?'

She gave an impatient shrug. 'It's probably best if I sleep in my own room.'

'You really think that's going to help?'

'Help what?' she shot back with a scowling frown.

Was she being deliberately obtuse?

'Help *us*,' Zac said patiently. 'This walking on eggshells tension.' He had visions of a twenty-two-hour flight back to Australia without resolving whatever bugged her.

At least Chloe gave a faint nod, as if she acknowledged this, then she leaned her back against the door and folded her arms over her chest and speared him with her nut-brown gaze. 'So you're saying that you need to talk about our relationship—or rather our lack of a relationship?'

'Well, from my experience, talking things over is usually what girls want.'

She smiled. Damn, even when the smile was glum, she looked incredibly lovely when she smiled. Zac had to work hard to curb his impulse to cross the room and haul her into his arms. He wanted to relight those wild flames again. Taste her lips, her skin, feel her going wild with him. Hell, how could he ever forget that blazing encounter?

How could he forget how much he'd loved having her around on a twenty-four hour basis? He'd never met a girl he felt so comfortable with. Until he'd wrecked things with his clumsy proposal, sharing his personal life with Chloe had felt so unexpectedly *right*...as if their personalities slotted magically together like one of those Chinese puzzles...

'So what do you think we need to talk about?' Chloe asked.

'To be honest, I'm not totally sure, but it sure as hell can't happen if you're on the other side of that wall.'

Now she lifted her hands in a gesture of surrender. 'OK. No big deal. I'll stay here. I'm actually very tired, though.'

'The talk's not mandatory,' he said, feeling ridiculously relieved by this small victory.

Nevertheless, after they both got into their separate beds, he could see, via the faint glow of Lucy's night light, that Chloe remained, as he was, lying on her back with her hands beneath her head, staring up at the ceiling.

It wasn't long before her voice reached him through the darkness. 'So what do you want to talk about?'

There was no mistaking the distrust in her tone.

Zac couldn't help smiling to himself. 'I thought I was supposed to ask that question.'

'But I've already told you. I don't have any issues. I'm perfectly fine.'

This was patently not true. Since they'd arrived back from the park Chloe had been tearing about like a wound-up toy on top speed.

'But I must admit I don't understand *you*,' she said next.

Zac had heard this comment before from women. Had heard it with regular monotony, if he was honest.

'I mean,' Chloe went on in that earnest way of hers, 'I don't understand why you're so convinced that falling in love is nothing but a fairy tale.'

She wasn't going to let go of this. Clearly, it was at the heart of her tension.

'Well, OK,' he said smoothly. 'Convince me otherwise. I'm assuming you have a vast experience of falling in love?'

'I don't know about vast,' she said. 'But I was certainly in love with my fiancé.'

Whack.

Zac's smugness vanished as surprise juddered through

him like a jack-hammer. How had he never known about her fiancé? More importantly, why hadn't Chloe said something about this guy when she so quickly and force-fully rejected his proposal?

Although he'd tried to make light of her rejection, her loud and clear *no* had stung. Zac had felt as if he was standing at the door of Aladdin's Cave, where the glit-tering riches and jewels represented a chance for a life-time's happiness and contentment.

Heaven help him, he'd actually pictured a home with Chloe and Lucy and then, just when this dream was within his reach, the portcullis had slammed down, cut-ting him off from his vision of happiness.

Now, he said, 'I/...I didn't realise you were engaged.'

'I'm not any more,' Chloe said softly. 'My fiancé died.'

Another shock. Despite the hotel's perfectly con-trolled heating, Zac was suddenly cold. 'Hell. I'm sorry. I had no idea.'

'I wouldn't expect you to know. It happened before I started working for you.'

'Right.' He swallowed uncomfortably as he absorbed this news.

Lying there in the dark beside her, it occurred to him that his assumptions about his PA had been en-tirely based on the image she presented at the office, but over the past few days that image had been crumbling and now it was blasted clear out of the water. 'Is it OK to ask what happened?'

After a small silence she said, 'Sam was a soldier—a Special Forces soldier. He was killed in Afghanistan.'

Zac swore and then quickly apologised. But this was almost one surprise too many. Special Forces soldiers were so damn tough and daring—the most highly skilled—which meant that Chloe had been about to marry a real life hero. 'I had no idea,' he said lamely.

'I don't like to talk about it.'

'No, I guess it must be hard.'

From the bed beside him, he heard a heavy sigh.

'I was a complete mess when it happened,' she said. 'That's why I came home to live with my parents. I didn't want to go out like other young people. I just wanted to hide away and…and grieve. I guess it wasn't exactly a healthy reaction.'

'But understandable.'

He heard the rustle of sheets as Chloe rolled to face him. 'Anyway, for what it's worth, I did love Sam. For me it was very real, an inescapable emotion. I suppose it was an attraction of opposites, but it worked for us. We were very happy and we had big plans for a family and everything.'

'That's…great…'

Zac had no idea what to say, but thinking about Chloe and her soldier made him feel inexplicably jealous… and depressed…

Inadequate, too. He understood now why Chloe had rejected him. She thought he merely wanted a mother for Lucy.

Damn it, he should have tried to express his feelings more truthfully but, chances were, anything he offered now would be a very poor second best to her true romance with her heroic soldier.

And if he tried to tell her how he really felt, how his days were always brighter when she was around, how, even at home in Brisbane, the weekends so often dragged and he couldn't wait till Monday mornings to see her again, it would sound crazy, as if he was in love…

'Are you asleep, Zac?' Chloe's voice dragged him back from his gloomy musings.

'Sorry. Were you saying something?'

'Now I've spilled my story, I was asking about you. Are you still going to insist that you've never fallen in love?'

His mind flashed to that one time in his past when he'd been young and deeply in love, with his head full of dreams and his heart full of hope. Until…

No. He never talked about that. He'd worked hard to put it all behind him and he wasn't going there now.

Chloe, however, was waiting for his answer.

'Well, yeah, sure I've been in love,' he told her with a joviality he didn't really feel. 'Hundreds of times.'

This was met by silence… It was ages before Chloe spoke and then she said quietly, 'That's exactly the answer I expected from you.'

After that she rolled away with her back to him. 'Goodnight, Zac.'

Her fed-up tone left him with the strong conviction that their conversation hadn't helped either of them and he knew he was going to have trouble getting to sleep.

Damn. The last thing he wanted was to lie awake remembering Rebecca…or what was now far worse— wrestling with regrets about Chloe…

The flight was scheduled for midday and both Chloe and Zac were nervous about how Lucy would behave during the long hours that stretched ahead of them.

To their relief, their fears were unfounded. When Lucy was awake the flight attendants seemed to love fussing over her, and when she slept the droning hum of the plane's engines seemed to soothe her into a deeper slumber.

'She's gorgeous and such a good baby,' several of the female passengers told Chloe. 'You're so lucky.' Chloe could tell from the way their eyes wandered that they considered Zac to be a major component of this luck.

Of course, Chloe thanked them and once again she didn't try to explain that she was neither Lucy's mother nor Zac's wife. But afterwards…she had to try to ignore the gnawing hollowness inside her, the annoying regret and second thoughts that had plagued her ever since she'd turned down Zac's proposal of marriage.

She knew she was going to miss Lucy terribly. In these few short days, she'd lost her heart to the baby. She'd grown to adore her, to love the feel and the smell of her, to love her bright curious eyes and hungry little mouth. When Zac wasn't looking, she'd even given Lucy little baby massages, following the instructions she'd read in one of the magazines.

As for Zac…despite the many strict lectures she'd de-livered to herself, she felt desperately miserable when-ever she thought about the end of this journey…when they went their separate ways. She'd grown so used to being with him twenty-four hours a day, to sharing meals with him, sharing middle of the night attempts to calm Lucy, listening to him in those quieter moments when he'd felt a need to talk a little more about Liv.

As for making love with him…Chloe's thoughts were seriously undisciplined when it came to *that* subject. She spent far too much time torturing herself by recalling every raunchy detail of going to bed with Zac…before firmly reminding herself it would never happen again.

'A penny for your thoughts.'

Chloe blushed. 'Excuse me?'

Zac leaned closer. 'You had your worried look, Ms Meadows. I wondered what was bothering you.'

She had no idea what to say. 'Um…I wasn't thinking about anything in particular.'

'Lucky you,' Zac murmured, leaning closer still.

'Why am I lucky?'

'You're not being tormented the way I am. I can't stop thinking about how much I want to kiss you.'

'Zac, don't be crazy. You can't start kissing on a plane.' Was he no longer bothered that she'd rejected his proposal?

'Why not?' he asked with that winning smile of his. 'They've dimmed the lights and no one's looking.'

So tempting…

'You want to, don't you?'

'No,' Chloe whispered, but she knew she didn't sound very convincing. No doubt because it wasn't the truth. She wanted nothing more.

When Zac leaned even closer and touched his lips to her cheek, she felt her whole body break into a smile. Instinctively, she closed her eyes and turned to him so her lips and his were almost touching. He needed no further invitation. His mouth brushed over hers in a teasing whisper-soft kiss that sent warm coils of pleasure spiralling deep. Chloe let her lips drift open and she welcomed the slide of his tongue.

'Mmm…' With a soft sound of longing, she moved as close to him as possible, kissing him harder…losing herself in the strength and the taste and the smell of him.

'I love you,' he whispered and wave after wave of happiness welled inside her. Everything was all right

after all. It was OK to love Zac. There was no reason
to hold back.

She slipped one hand behind his neck to anchor herself and then she nudged her leg against his, as she was
seized by a hot and feverish longing to climb into his lap.

'Chloe?'

Zac's questioning voice sounded quite loudly in her
ear.

Chloe blinked. Her head was on Zac's shoulder. Her
hand was curled around his nape. Her knee was hooked
over his thigh. When she pulled back to check his face,
he was staring at her with a strangely puzzled smile.

'What happened?' she asked.

'I think you fell asleep.'

Oh, my God. Had she been dreaming?

Cheeks burning with embarrassment, Chloe whipped
her hand away and swerved back into her seat. 'I…I'm
so sorry. I have no idea how that happened.' With a soft
moan she sank her face into her hands.

'Hey, don't worry,' she heard him say. 'I'm already
wishing I didn't wake you up.'

Chloe lowered her hands from her face. 'How long
was I—?'

'Climbing all over me?'

She cringed. 'Yeah.'

'Only about ten minutes or so. I'd say there were only
about a dozen people who walked past.'

She stared at him in horror. 'They saw me?'

But Zac was grinning hard now and she realised he
was teasing her. She gave his arm a punch. 'You're a
lying rat, Zac Corrigan.'

Her embarrassment lingered, however. Even if half
the people in the cabin hadn't seen her draping herself

all over Zac, *he* knew all about it. She thanked her lucky stars that he hadn't pushed her for a proper explanation. But what must he be thinking?

They were finally flying over Australian soil, although it would still be several hours before they touched down in Brisbane.

Chloe had just come back from the changing room with Lucy, and Zac was waiting with the heated bottle the flight attendant had delivered.

'Do you want to do the honours?' Chloe asked him.

'Sure.' He held out his arms for the baby and Chloe's heart had a minor meltdown as she watched the tender way he smiled at his niece.

'You know,' he said, as he settled Lucy in his arms and carefully tipped the teat into her eager little mouth, 'I hate to think about trying to do this on my own when I get home. It won't be the same without your help.'

Chloe closed her eyes against the pang of dismay his comment aroused. She was going to miss this, too, more than she could possibly have imagined. When she opened her eyes again, the sight of Zac and Lucy together was beyond gorgeous.

In moments like this, the temptation to retract her rejection of Zac's proposal was huge…until she remembered that he only wanted her because she was good with Lucy…and possibly because their chemistry was undeniably hot. Was she crazy to believe these reasons weren't enough?

She thought about Sam and the way he'd made her feel and the many ways he'd showed her that he cared…just through little things like gifts or a surprise invitation, or the way he held her close. Of course, those gestures weren't all that different from Zac's behaviour, really. And the annoying thing was there were times when she felt even closer to Zac than she ever had with Sam.

Truth to tell, during the two years Chloe had known Sam, he'd spent a good proportion of the time on deployment in Afghanistan. So she was certainly better acquainted with Zac, with his good and bad habits, his strengths, hopes and fears. His belief that love was an illusion…

This thought sobered Chloe. 'You'll find some other woman to help you,' she said.

'Not straight away. That will take time to arrange.'

'Well, yes, I doubt that even you could manage to pull off a wedding inside a week, Zac. You'll need to hire a sitter or a nanny for the interim.'

'And that won't be easy in the week between Christmas and New Year.'

Chloe slid him a sideways glance. 'You'll manage.'

'So you wouldn't consider it?' he asked, trapping her once again with his clear grey gaze.

'Consider what, exactly?'

'Helping me out for a few more days?'

She should have seen this coming, should have been prepared, but she'd thought, after her rejection, that Zac would back right off.

'Chloe?'

'I don't know,' she said. 'I'm thinking.'

'I've plenty of bedrooms,' he went on, offering one of his customary coaxing smiles. 'You could have your own room and we could put Lucy in the room next door to you.'

'Where would you be?'

'Just down the hall a bit.' Now he had the cheek to

grin at her. 'Safely out of your way, but near enough to be on call to help with Lucy.'

If she thought about it rationally, without her silly emotions getting in the way, his request was probably reasonable. As long as this wasn't the thin end of the wedge…

'So what's your plan, Zac? You're still planning to… to…get married, aren't you?'

Chloe saw an unreadable flicker in his eyes, but his face was deadpan. 'I still think that's the preferable option.'

'And Marissa's the preferable candidate?'

'I guess so, yes.' His tone suggested that he still needed to give this serious thought. 'But I know I'll have important groundwork to do before I can convince her. At the moment, I don't even know if she's still available.'

'So it could take some time…'

Zac set the baby's bottle on the tray table while he gently lifted Lucy onto his shoulder to help her to bring up her wind. 'I wouldn't expect you to stay at my place for too long, Chloe. Just for a night or two, till I get my bearings.'

'My parents might—'

'Your parents are welcome to stay on at the hotel, as long as they're enjoying it.'

'Oh, they're enjoying it all right.'

'Then, would you consider it?'

The last thing Chloe needed was more time in Zac's company. What she needed was distance. Time and space to regroup and to clear herself of her tangled thoughts and emotions. But then she looked at Lucy. Zac had shifted her onto his lap and she was curled over his big hand as he gently rubbed her back. She was such a dear little thing and she looked so cute now.

'I wonder if Marissa likes babies,' she found herself saying.

Zac lifted a dark eyebrow. 'I have no idea. I guess that's one of the many things I'll have to ask her.'

Chloe had never been to Zac's penthouse apartment, perched high in an inner city tower block. He'd project-managed its construction and it was a striking piece of architecture with views up and down the Brisbane River—all very shiny and modern with high gloss timber floors, large expanses of glass and a flashy granite and stainless steel kitchen.

By the time they'd emerged from Customs it was too late to try to go shopping for baby gear, so they went straight to Zac's place and made a snug nest for Lucy by pushing two black leather lounge chairs together and then lining the space with a quilt.

'She looks impossibly tiny, doesn't she?' Lucy said as they stood looking down at her.

'Yeah.' Zac reached down and softly stroked Lucy's dark hair. 'Welcome home, tiny girl.'

The love shining in his eyes brought a lump to Chloe's throat. Then he straightened and his eyes were still shiny as he smiled at Chloe.

'There's a restaurant downstairs,' he said. 'I could send down for a takeaway meal.'

'I'm not especially hungry.' She would blame jet lag for her low mood, but from the moment she'd arrived she'd felt on the verge of tears.

'Maybe just one serving to share?' Zac suggested. 'Something light? They do great chilli prawns.'

Which was how they ended up on that first night, sitting on his balcony with a fresh breeze blowing up the river, eating chilli prawns and washing it down with a glass of white wine, while they enjoyed the city lights.

'You must love living here,' Chloe commented as she watched pretty ladders of light stretch across the smooth surface of the river.

'It's been great,' Zac admitted. 'At least it's been very handy for a bachelor.'

'Party Central?'

'At times, yes.' But Zac was frowning. 'I'm not sure I'd like to stay here with Lucy. She'll need a backyard with swings and other kids in her street to play with.'

'That safe suburban life you dream of,' Chloe suggested with a tired smile.

'Exactly.'

'Do you think you'll find it hard to adapt to that kind of life?'

'I guess that depends on who I can convince to come and live with us,' he said quietly and there was just enough light for Chloe to see the way his gaze flashed in her direction.

Without warning, her throat was choked and her eyes were stinging, spilling tears.

'Chloe.'

She threw up her hands. 'It's just jet lag. I need to hit the sack.' Already she was on her feet. 'Thanks for the prawns, Zac. They were delicious.'

'Don't get up when Lucy wakes,' he called after her. 'I'm not too tired. I'll be fine.'

'OK, thanks.' She kept her tear-stained face averted. 'See you in the morning. Goodnight.'

Of course, after that, Chloe took ages to get to sleep. She tossed and turned and agonised about Zac, but when she finally nodded off she slept deeply and soundly. She woke to find bright daylight streaming through the crack between her curtains and from below she could hear the sounds of city traffic.

Feeling guilty about spending an entire night without helping, she sprang out of bed and hurried to the lounge room, but the baby wasn't in her makeshift cot.

Chloe shot a hasty glance to the kitchen. An empty baby's bottle stood on the granite counter, but there was no other sign that Zac had been up and she couldn't hear any sounds from within the apartment. Quickly she dashed back to her room to check the time. It was only just coming up to six o'clock, much earlier than she'd expected, but of course the sun rose super-early in Brisbane in midsummer.

And where was Lucy?

She tiptoed down the hallway towards Zac's room, then stood listening for Lucy's snuffles and snorts.

Nothing.

She knew it was silly to panic, but where Lucy was concerned her imagination leapt into overdrive. Something had happened. Lucy was ill. Zac had rushed with her to a twenty-four-hour medical centre.

Having thoroughly alarmed herself, she dashed into Zac's bedroom. And came to a skidding halt.

He was sound asleep, lying on his back. And Lucy was in the bed beside him, while another empty baby's bottle stood on the bedside table.

Chloe found herself transfixed as she looked down at them—the great big man and the tiny baby girl. Zac had kicked the sheet off and he was only wearing a pair of black silk boxer shorts, which allowed her a perfect opportunity to admire his broad bare chest, his muscular arms and shoulders, the smattering of dark hair narrowing down to the waistband of his shorts.

She couldn't help reliving her amazing experience of being up close and personal with that toned and golden body.

'Morning.'

His deep voice startled her. She'd been so busy ogling him, she hadn't noticed that he'd woken.

'I...I was just checking to see where Lucy was,' she stammered.

Zac grinned sleepily. His eyes were mere silver slits, but she knew he'd caught her checking him out. Then he sat up, scrubbed a hand over his face and blinked at the baby beside him. 'I didn't mean to bring her back here, but with the jet lag and everything...' He frowned as he leaned closer to check the tiny sleeping girl. Her tummy was moving softly up and down as she breathed. 'Thank God I didn't roll on her.'

'When's she due for another feed?' Chloe was eager now to shoulder her share of the duties.

Zac squinted at the bedside clock. 'I'd say in about another hour.'

'You should go back to sleep then. If she wakes I'll deal with her.'

'Sounds great. Thanks.' He was smiling as he flopped back onto the bed.

As she left Zac's room, Chloe hoped he hadn't been keeping tabs on her recent 'lapses'. First there'd been her attempt to climb all over him in the plane, then her tears last night, and now this morning's ogling. Surely these added up to highly inappropriate behaviour from a girl who had flatly rejected him?

* * *

It was a difficult day. They had to drag themselves around while their body clocks readjusted, and between snatches of sleep they made phone calls. Chloe rang her parents and Zac rang Marissa. His phone call took ages. Chloe had no idea what transpired and her curiosity was killing her but Zac chose not to tell her, which was appropriate, of course, now that she was simply his PA again. In the afternoon they went shopping for the necessary baby gear.

They aimed for an early night and fortunately Lucy co-operated. While Chloe put through a load of washing, Zac cooked their dinner, making a fair fist of grilling steaks on the balcony barbecue. He served them with mushrooms and beans and they ate the meal outside again, enjoying the warm evening and the city lights.

'Wow,' said Chloe as she tucked in. 'This is delicious, Zac. You've put lemon and chilli on the beans, haven't you? And some kind of herb on the mushrooms?'

He ducked his head towards the attractive cluster of potted herbs on his balcony. 'I sprinkled a little thyme over them.'

'Hmm.' Chloe speared a succulent mushroom with her fork. 'I think I've uncovered a dark horse, Zachary Corrigan.'

'What makes you say that?'

'You're actually a closet chef.'

He lifted a gorgeous black eyebrow.

'You are, aren't you, Zac?'

This brought an embarrassed smile. 'Closet chef? That's a big statement to make after sampling one hasty meal.'

'Hasty or not, this meal is sensational.' Chloe sliced

off a tender corner of steak. 'But I actually have further evidence. I checked out your pantry and fridge.'

'When?'

'While I was stowing away Lucy's formula.'

'So you've been spying on me?'

'I couldn't resist a little snooping. Sorry, it's a bad habit of mine, but I have a thing about fridges and pantries. You see, they tell so much about a person—in the kitchen, at least. And, well, I noticed you keep a French brand of Parmesan and an Italian brand of risotto, and you have all these bottles of Thai and Vietnamese sauces and about three different types of olive oil...'

'So?'

'Zac, you know very well that only a serious cook would bother.'

'I like to eat.' He shrugged. 'And cooking's actually relaxing...'

Relaxing? This was such a surprise Chloe laughed. 'And here I was, imagining that you ate out every night.'

'No way. Only every second night.'

They smiled at each other across the table. It was a smile of friendship and understanding and...something far deeper...which made Chloe feel all shivery and confused again.

'Do you like to cook?' Zac asked her.

'Well, I usually cook for my parents, but they only like very plain food like shepherd's pie or—' She stopped. This conversation was becoming far too intimate. It was making her feel closer to Zac when she was supposed to be stepping away.

CHAPTER ELEVEN

CHLOE WAS GIVING Lucy her bath when Zac left, shortly after breakfast.

'See you later,' he said, ducking his head around the bathroom doorway.

Unhappily guessing that he was heading off to see Marissa, Chloe forced brightness into her voice. 'You might heighten your luck if you take her flowers and chocolate.'

Zac frowned. 'I guess…'

'Marissa likes Oriental lilies and ginger chocolate.'

'How do you know these things?' he asked, but then he gave a soft humourless laugh. 'Don't tell me. It's all on a spreadsheet.'

'Naturally.' Chloe wished him luck but, as soon as she heard the apartment's front door close behind him, her face crumpled and she was overwhelmed by the most devastating, painful loss.

Zac was gone. She'd thrown away her very last opportunity and this was the end.

She felt cold all over as she scooped the baby out of the water and wrapped her in a fluffy bath towel.

'Oh, God, Lucy,' she whispered. 'You know what I've done, don't you? I've just thrown away the chance to be your mummy. And I've lost my very last opportunity to be with Zac.'

A terrible ache bloomed in her chest as she hugged Lucy to her and breathed in the scent of her clean baby skin. 'Honestly, Luce, I was only trying to be sensible. I can't marry a man who doesn't even know if he loves me.'

But how could I have known that being sensible and letting him go would still break my heart?

Misery washed through her, as cold and bleak as when she'd lost Sam. *S*he carried Lucy through to the spare bedroom, now designated as the baby's nursery, and laid her gently on the new changing table, part of the furniture she and Zac had bought yesterday. Carefully, she patted the baby's skin dry and sprinkled and smoothed talcum powder into her creases. She picked up one of the tiny singlets and slipped it over Lucy's head, before angling her arms through the holes.

Luckily, she'd done this many times now because the entire time she worked her mind was miles away. With Zac. She was picturing his arrival at Marissa's, making his charming apologies or doing whatever was necessary to placate her, and then inviting her out. They would probably go to the beach. Chloe could imagine them walking hand in hand along the sand at the water's edge, or having a drink at a bar overlooking the sea. Zac would be at his alluring best as he explained the sad situation that had left him with Lucy. By the time he'd finished, Marissa would be putty in his hands.

Of course she would want to marry him.

And Chloe couldn't bear it. Couldn't bear to think that Zac would marry a woman he didn't love—and who probably didn't love him, simply to provide a mother for Lucy. How could he be such a fool?

She finished dressing the baby and took her through to the kitchen to collect a bottle of formula from the fridge. As she waited for it to heat, she paced restlessly, agonising over her own foolishness. And Zac's foolishness, too.

Surely he was deceiving himself when he claimed that he didn't believe in love? For heaven's sake, she only had to think back over the past few days to see all kinds of evidence of Zac's love in action.

He'd gone above and beyond the call of mere duty for Liv and for Lucy, but he'd also gone out of his way for Chloe as well. Not just with lovely gifts like the bracelet and the Christmas banquet, although she knew these were more personal and special than the gifts Zac usually bestowed on his women—but, beyond that, he'd also been thoughtful and considerate and kind. And fun.

Both in and out of bed…

Chloe wondered now, too late, if she should have given Zac a chance to explain his vision of the marriage he'd proposed. She'd simply jumped to conclusions and assumed he would continue to play the field.

But if she thought about the past week, when she'd been with him day and night, she couldn't really fault his behaviour. Actually, if anyone had misbehaved, she had. She'd practically thrown herself into his arms on that day they'd made love.

Now, as she went back to the kitchen to collect the heated bottle, she was more depressed than ever. She couldn't believe she'd brought this pain on herself and she'd thrown everything away because she'd needed to hear three stupid words from Zac. Hadn't she known all along that words were easy? Actions carried so much more weight…and Zac's actions had said so much… but now she'd lost him and she had no one to blame but herself.

'I hope I don't weep all over you,' she told Lucy as she settled in an armchair to feed her. 'I don't want to upset you. Don't take any notice of me, will you, darling? I'll try to stop thinking about him.'

It was impossible to turn her thoughts off, of course. She figured that by now Zac would be well on his way to the Gold Coast—too far down the expressway for her to phone him with some weak excuse that would bring him back. She had tried to be sensible one time too many, and as a result she felt as bereft and as heartbroken as she had when she lost Sam.

And Lucy had already finished her bottle.

'Sorry!' Chloe felt all kinds of guilty as she set the bottle aside and lifted Lucy to her shoulder. She hadn't been paying attention and she'd let the baby feed too quickly. Now the poor darling would probably be in pain.

Chloe stood, hoping that a little walking up and down would do the trick, but she was only halfway across the lounge room when the doorbell rang.

'Who on earth could this be?' she complained, sounding scarily like her mother, and as she went to open the door she dashed a hand to her face and hoped it wasn't too obvious that she'd been crying.

A young woman stood on the doorstep—a very pretty young woman with long blonde hair and the kind of slender figure that came from living on lettuce leaves and very little else. She was wearing strong perfume, tight floral jeans and a tiny tight top that revealed a toned and tanned midriff, as well as a silver navel ring.

The girl's jaw dropped when she saw Chloe and Lucy. 'Who are you?' she demanded.

'Are you looking for Zac?' Chloe asked in response.

'Yes. What's happened to him?' The girl looked genuinely worried. 'He just took off and he's been away for the whole of Christmas.'

'There was a family emergency and he had to rush to London.' Chloe felt obliged to explain this, even though she had no idea who this girl was. She certainly wasn't one of Zac's regulars. 'Zac's sister died,' she said.

The girl frowned, clearly struggling to take this in. 'That's sad. So are you a relative then?'

'No, I'm Zac's PA and this is his little niece, Lucy.'

'His PA? I think you rang Zac last week. Yes, it was you, wasn't it? And then he went racing off.'

'Yes, it was all terribly sudden.' Chloe realised this had to be the girl who'd answered Zac's phone on that fateful Wednesday night. She'd pretended to be answering from a Chinese takeaway.

'I'm sorry to hear about his sister,' the girl said.

'It was terrible,' Chloe agreed just as Lucy pulled up her knees and began to wail loudly.

'I take it Zac's not here now?' The girl raised her voice to be heard above Lucy.

'No. I'm not sure when he'll be back.'

'I guess I'll just have to keep trying his mobile then.'

'I'm not sure that's a good idea,' Chloe responded hastily. 'Not today. He's…he's still very busy.'

The girl pouted. 'Well, can you at least tell him that Daisy called?'

'Of course I can, Daisy. I won't forget. Nice to meet you.'

Lucy was distraught as Chloe closed the door. 'Oh,

sweetheart, I'm so sorry.' She began to pace, jiggling the baby gently. 'I'm afraid I know how you feel. I want to wail along with you.'

Back in the lounge room, she tried sitting with Lucy in her lap. Zac had perfected the art of burping her this way and Chloe willed herself to forget about her own woes and to concentrate on comforting the baby. She was rewarded by a massive burp.

'Oh, wow! Good girl. Aren't you clever?' She kissed the baby's downy head and cuddled her close and she sat there for a while, enjoying the warmth and snuggling closeness. But she was close to tears again as she took Lucy back to her brand new cot and tucked her in. She set the teddy bear that Liv had bought where Lucy could see it and then she tiptoed away.

From the doorway she looked back. 'I'm going to miss you so much.'

She waited for an answering wail, but the baby remained silent. When Chloe stole back into the room to double-check, Lucy's eyes were already closed. Chloe went back to the lounge room and collected the empty bottle, took it through to the kitchen...

Now what?

Unfortunately, the answer came almost immediately. Her next task was to write her letter of resignation.

She gave an agonised groan as this thought hit home. But she had no choice. It had to be done. She couldn't continue as Zac's PA now that she'd become so intimately involved in his personal life. She cared too much about Lucy *and* about Zac and she would care too much about the personal choices Zac made in the future.

And how could she pretend that their blazing lovemaking wouldn't always be there between them? A teasing, haunting memory. How could she ever forget that amazing spontaneity and passion? Heavens, if she stayed in Zac's office, she might find herself hoping it could happen again.

For that reason alone, she had no choice but to leave. It would be untenable for her to continue working for Zac after he was married to Marissa.

She hoped he would see that, too.

She should act immediately, draft a resignation now and have it ready for when he returned. She could type it on her phone, could even email it straight to Zac. With luck, he would accept it without too much argument.

It was so hard, though… Chloe felt sick as she started to type.

She began with *Dear Mr Corrigan,* then deleted it and replaced it with *Dear Zac.* Her hands were shaking, her thumbs fumbling on the keys as she forced herself to continue.

It is with deep regret…

Again she stopped and deleted. She had to keep this businesslike.

I wish to advise that I am resigning from my position as Personal Assistant to the Managing Director of ZedCee Management Consultants.

The terms of my contract require two weeks' notice for the termination of employment from either party. I will make myself available to assist in a smooth transition for my replacement.

Chloe pressed her hand against the new ache that flared just beneath her ribs, then she continued to type…

I've enjoyed working at…

She stopped and let out another soft groan. What was the point of telling Zac that? He knew only too well how much she'd loved her job. Better to just ask him for a reference.

Did she want a reference? She supposed she should have one, but she hated the thought of having to hunt for another job…

As she began to type again she heard a noise… Once again, it was coming from the front door…

Another caller?

This time there was the unmistakable sound of a key turning in the lock…

Not another of Zac's girlfriends? Chloe wasn't sure she could face another of Zac's blonde beauties. And it seemed that this one had privileged status and her very own key.

Wincing as she set her half-written letter aside, Chloe got to her feet. Her *bare* feet.

She couldn't remember the last time she'd checked her appearance in a mirror and there was every chance she had baby dribble on her T-shirt, and if this woman had a key she was sure to be at least as glamorous as Daisy. Chloe was madly finger-combing her hair as she heard footsteps coming down the hallway. She braced herself for a vision of sexy high fashion.

She had the words ready. 'I'm sorry, but Zac isn't—'
The figure coming into the lounge room was tall and

dark and exceptionally masculine. Chloe's heart almost stopped.

'Zac?'

'Hi.' He dropped his keys into a pottery dish on the low entertainment unit, and then he set down a pot of bright red double gerberas and a box of chocolates. He looked pale, almost unwell, and deep lines furrowed his brow and the sides of his mouth.

'What happened?' Chloe had visions of a highway smash. 'Is everything all right? Did you get as far as the Gold Coast?'

'No.' Zac stood in the middle of the room with his hands on his hips. His chest expanded as he drew a deep breath.

Something had clearly gone wrong. Had Marissa refused to see him?

'Is there anything I can do? A cup of—'

A faint sad smile briefly tilted a corner of his mouth. 'All I need is for you to listen, Chloe. There's—' his Adam's apple rippled as he swallowed '—there's something I need to tell you.'

The growing knots of anxiety in Chloe's stomach tightened as Zac turned, looked around his lounge room, almost as if he was seeing it for the first time. Then he took a seat in the chair opposite her, and he leaned back against the smooth leather upholstery as if this could somehow help him to relax.

He was wearing jeans and a white shirt, unbuttoned at the collar and with the sleeves rolled back. Despite the crackling tension, Chloe couldn't help admiring the way his dark hair and bronzed skin contrasted so gorgeously with the whiteness of his shirt.

'I hope you haven't had more bad news,' she said gently.

'No, just a painful revelation.' Again, he cracked the faintest glimmer of a smile, before he dropped his gaze and traced the arm of the chair with his fingertips, as if he was testing the texture of the leather.

Chloe tried not to notice how beautiful his hands were, so long-fingered and strong, and she struggled to banish unhelpful memories of his hands touching and caressing her, driving her to rapture.

'I didn't go to the Gold Coast,' he said. 'Actually, I have a confession. Almost as soon as I dialled Marissa's number yesterday, I knew that proposing to her would be a huge mistake, but then I had to spend the next hour coming up with a crazy explanation for why I'd rung her...and then more time trying to wriggle out of seeing her again.' He gave a wry smile as he shook his head. 'It was yet another of my famous stuff-ups.'

Chloe swallowed nervously, unsure what to say.

'I'm sorry I gave you the wrong impression, Chloe. I should have set you straight this morning when you mentioned the flowers, but I wasn't ready to explain.'

'It's not really my business.'

Zac smiled at her then. 'Of course, Ms Meadows.' Then his expression was serious once more as he said, 'Truth is, I've been walking the streets, trying to clear my head and think everything through.'

Chloe nodded. This was understandable. He'd had next to no privacy in the past few days.

'You asked me in London if I've ever been in love,' he said next, somewhat abruptly.

In an instant her skin turned to goosebumps. 'Yes, I did.'

'I said I hadn't, but I lied.'

Oh. Chloe couldn't think what to say, but her heart had begun to pound so loudly now that she was sure Zac must be able to hear it.

'I was in love once, a long time ago,' he went on quietly. 'It was in my first year at university.' His shoulders lifted in a shrug. 'I guess it was first love, or puppy love, or whatever, but it certainly felt real at the time.' He looked away to the far window and its views of the sunny city skyline. 'Her name was Rebecca and I was crazy about her.'

Chloe had no idea why Zac had come back with flowers or why he was telling her this, and she certainly couldn't risk trying to guess, but she was so tense now she thought she might snap in two.

'Of course, I had all these dreams,' he went on. 'Nothing flash. Just the usual—marriage, family, happy ever after…'

The things he no longer believed in.

'Then my parents disappeared,' he said. 'And my life changed overnight. I felt I had to give up university and get a job, and take on the responsibility of looking after Liv. I needed to be home for her on the weekends and in the evenings. I didn't have time for a social life, so I put my dreams on the back burner.'

'And you broke up with Rebecca,' Chloe guessed.

'Yes.' He gave another crookedly cynical smile. 'She soon took up with another guy and within two years she married him.'

Oh, dear.

Chloe could see it all so clearly… Zac's world had been turned upside down when his parents disappeared... He'd sacrificed his dreams, only to be rewarded by heartbreak...

But as she sat there, listening and watching him and not daring to analyse why he was telling her this, she realised something so surprising that she gasped and felt quite giddy...

Surely, Zac's whole playboy persona had been a reaction to this heartbreak? After he'd lost his parents and his first girlfriend—a girl he'd genuinely loved—he'd been desperate to save his little sister. But then Liv had proved rebellious and Zac had responded with his own form of rebellion—his never-ending procession of *Foolish Females*.

Playing the field had been Zac's way of escaping, of protecting himself from ever being hurt again...

Of course it was far safer to never fall in love. Chloe knew this only too well. She'd been doing the same thing in a different way. After Sam's death, she'd avoided a social life, with its accompanying risks and pain, by hiding away and caring for her parents.

Oh, Zac. Her heart ached for him as she watched him now, as he drew another deep, nervous breath and let it out with a sigh.

She wondered if his current dilemma was her fault somehow. Had he realised that Marissa would also expect a declaration of love...and that, for him, it was still a step too far...

'So does this mean...?' she began, but then she stopped, uncertain of how to voice her thoughts diplomatically.

Zac looked across at her, not quite smiling. 'The long-winded point that I'm trying to make is that I do know what it's like to love someone and to lose her.'

'Yes, but that shouldn't—'

Chloe stopped again as the silent message in Zac's eyes made her heart thump so loudly she was sure he must hear it. She was poised on the edge of her seat now and she held her breath, not daring to say anything more, not daring to wonder, even fearfully, where exactly this revelation was heading.

Without warning, Zac launched to his feet again.

'I walked over the bridge and into the city,' he said. 'One of my mates is a real estate agent and I was going to ask him to look out for a place for Lucy and me.'

Chloe nodded miserably. Zac had decided to take responsibility for Lucy after all—without 'using' one of his women. It was an important step forward for him and she knew she should be pleased.

He forced an edgy smile, then turned and picked up the pot of red gerberas. 'I didn't get as far as my mate's office. I walked past a florist's.' The flowers trembled in Zac's hand. He was shaking and Chloe couldn't bear it.

'There were all these lilies in the window. You'd told me to get lilies for Marissa, but I suddenly knew: if I bought flowers for anyone, it had to be for you.'

She could barely hear him now over the ridiculous thundering of her heartbeats and it was almost impossible to see him through her tears.

'But I had no idea which were your favourites,' Zac said. 'I don't have a spreadsheet for you, Chloe.' He gave her another of his gorgeous crooked, sad smiles. 'But these made me think of your red dress and…and I hope you like them. Anyway, I had no choice. I had to bring them back to *you*.'

She was shaking, pressing a hand to her mouth…

'I was hoping to…to have another shot at that proposal.'

Now Chloe was on the edge of her seat, so tense she could only bite her lip as tears filled her eyes.

'I…I think I might have given you the impression last time that I only asked you to marry me because you would make a good mother for Lucy. And you would— you'd be perfect, but that's not why I need you, Chloe. That's so, so wrong.'

She swiped at her stupid, blinding tears. She wanted to see him—*needed* to see him. Oh, dear Lord, he looked so worried.

'The truth is,' Zac said, 'I reckon I've probably been in love with you since you first arrived in the office. I guess I just wouldn't let myself admit it, but I love being around you, Chloe. I love seeing you, whether you're serious or happy, or telling me off. I love hearing your voice. I love asking your advice. I even love drinking your damn cups of tea… I know it sounds crazy, but I hurry to work each day, just to see you.'

She thought of all those mornings that she'd looked forward to, too… Zac almost always arrived early, around the same time that she did and they always shared a little harmless light conversation. He would crack a joke, talk about something he'd heard on the news as he was driving to work, share a little gossip about one of their competitors. Drink the tea that she made.

Those mornings, before the rest of the staff arrived, had been her favourite time of day and now she could feel the truth of his claim filling her with light. Golden light was flooding her from the toes up, filling her chest, her arms, her head.

'No, it doesn't sound crazy,' she told him.

Zac swallowed. 'No?'

'I've felt the same about you.'

His eyes widened. 'You have?'

She felt brave enough to tell him now. 'Hopelessly in love from Day One. Probably ever since my job interview.'

For a trembling moment they stared at each other while this astonishing truth sank in. Then Zac set down the flowers and held out his arms and at last—at *last*—Chloe flew to safety.

As she hurled herself against him, his arms came around her, holding her preciously close. 'Oh, Chloe, I do love you. So, so much.'

'I know, I know.' She pressed her face against his shoulder, loving that she now had the right to be there, in his arms, leaning in to his strength.

'But I need to apologise about the way I carried on with the rubbish about romance and delusions,' Zac persisted. 'I was deluding myself. I *know* love's real. It's how I feel about you. Standing outside that florist's, I couldn't breathe when I realised I was losing you. I love you so much.'

He pulled back to look into her eyes. 'You do believe me, don't you?'

'I do, Zac.'

'Honestly?'

'You've already shown me in so many ways.'

'Oh, God, I hope so.'

There were no more tears now as she kissed his jaw, his cheek.

'Oh, Chloe.' Framing her face with his hands, Zac touched his lips to hers and his kiss was so tender and lingering and loving, Chloe thought she might actually swoon with an excess of happiness.

It was some time before their kiss ended and she nestled her head against his shoulder again. 'You were right,' she said. 'We don't need the words.'

He gave a soft laugh. 'But I want to say them now. I'm not scared of them and it feels so good. I'm going to tell you every day that I love you.' With gentle fingers, he traced the line of her cheek. 'Isn't it incredible that we've both been waiting? Why did it take us so damn long to work this out?'

'We're both sticklers for office protocol?'

This brought one of Zac's beautifully devilish grins and, a beat later, he slipped one arm around Chloe's shoulders, then a hand beneath her knees as he literally swept her off her feet. 'Stuff the protocol, Ms Meadows.'

He was already halfway to the bedroom.

EPILOGUE

AT FIRST, WHEN Chloe woke, she forgot what day it was. She lay very still with her eyes closed, enjoying the warm stream of the sunlight that filtered through the poinciana tree outside the bedroom window.

Then she rolled towards Zac, reaching for him…only to find an empty space in the bed. Her eyes flashed open and she saw their bedroom, bright with summer sunlight, saw the little silver tree on the dressing table, the red glass tumblers holding the tea light candles that she'd lit last night. She'd had so much fun decorating the house for Christmas.

Zap. She sat up with a jolt as she remembered. This was it. Christmas morning.

How on earth could she have slept in? She'd been looking forward to this day with an almost childish excitement.

Now there was no time to waste. She had to see if Lucy was awake and she needed to know what Zac was up to.

Throwing off the sheet, she smiled at her new Christmas pyjamas—a red T-shirt teamed with cotton pants decorated with bright green holly and red bows. Although Chloe had always loved Christmas, this year she'd probably gone a trifle overboard, with decorations in every room of the house as well as extra details like special tablecloths and napkins for their Christmas dinner. She'd even bought special festive coffee mugs. Luckily, Zac didn't seem to mind.

Now, she ducked into Lucy's room. 'Merry Christmas, baby g—'

The cot was empty and Chloe felt a stab of disappointment, but she quickly squashed it as the smell of coffee wafted from downstairs...and then, as she descended, she heard the deep rumbling voice that she knew so well...

'And this is a special ornament that Mummy bought last Christmas in Selfridges in London... You were there, too, you know, pumpkin. Such a teensy little thing you were then...and it was wintertime and cold, not sweltering and hot like today... And over here under the tree are all the lovely presents... No, no, hang on. You can't rip them to pieces just yet. We can't open them till Mummy wakes up...'

At the bottom of the stairs now, Chloe caught a glimpse through to the lounge room and she stopped to admire the view of Zac and Lucy together. Zac was balancing Lucy on his hip with the practised ease of an expert and the baby was chuckling and reaching up to grab at a bright decoration. When she couldn't reach, she tried to squeeze his nose instead.

In response, Zac ducked, then playfully pretended to nibble Lucy's hand, which made her squeal with delight.

Chloe grinned. She never tired of seeing these two together. Over the past year they had formed a very special bond that boded very well for the future.

Lucy had grown into such a cute little bundle of mischief. She was a sturdy and determined one-year-old, now, and her hair was a mass of glossy dark curls, her eyes a bright, vivid blue. And she was constantly breaking into the most wonderfully happy smiles.

In Zac's strong arms, however, she still looked small and vulnerable...but safe. So wonderfully safe.

'And up here is something incredibly important,' Zac told the little girl as he pointed to a bunch of greenery in the doorway. 'This is a VIP plant that I have to show your mummy. It's called mistletoe and it's a tradition. Your mum's very fond of tradition...'

Chloe smiled again and felt a flush of pure, unfiltered joy. Soon it would all begin—the exchange of presents, the feasting, and sharing the day with her parents...

It would be quite a simple Christmas compared with last year's cathedral and banquet, but for Chloe this felt like the perfect end to a year that had been wonderful in so many ways—bringing happiness beyond her wildest dreams. At times it had seemed almost too good to be true and she'd had to pinch herself.

Of course, the three hundred and sixty-five days since their Christmas in London hadn't been a total bed of roses. In fact, the year had started off quite busily, and Chloe had spent most of January learning to balance caring for Lucy with helping a new PA to settle into her job.

Zac had been worried that Chloe might be bored with staying at home full-time and so they'd experimented with hiring a babysitter, who minded Lucy for one day a week while Chloe worked on the ZedCee files from her home office. It had worked well. Chloe loved being Lucy's mum, but she also found it rewarding to keep in touch with projects that had nothing to do with nappies or feeding schedules.

Then, in March, they'd moved out of the inner city apartment and into their contemporary two-storey home in the leafy suburb of Kenmore. They'd had a ton of fun house-hunting together, and they loved this house. With Zac's assistance, Chloe's parents were resettled two blocks away, in a lovely cottage in a retirement complex.

Chloe visited them almost every day, often walking there and taking Lucy for an outing in the pram. The little girl loved her Grammy and Gramps, and of course Hettie and Joe Meadows were utterly smitten by the baby, and they were completely shameless about their hero worship of Zac.

The wedding had been in June. Zac and Chloe had chosen a simple ceremony on the beach with a select group of friends and Chloe's misty-eyed parents. Afterwards, Zac and Chloe had flown north to Hamilton Island and, naturally, they'd taken Lucy with them. It was all quite magical.

There'd been tough days too, of course, times when Zac's grief for Liv had caught up with him, but it helped that Chloe had been through her own dark days of grief and she understood.

She'd been worried when Lucy's first birthday drew near, knowing that it coincided with a very sad anniversary. But six days ago the three of them had taken the ferry across to Stradbroke Island and there, while Lucy crawled on the sand and tried to chase tiny crabs, Chloe had watched as Zac paddled alone on a surfboard, out beyond the breakers. He'd taken a bunch of yellow roses and the small urn with Liv's ashes...

Afterwards, they'd stayed on the beach, playing with Lucy and talking quietly, remembering their journey to London...and Zac had shared one or two memories of Liv...

Eventually, Lucy had fallen asleep in Zac's arms and so they'd stayed there, sitting together on the warm sand and watching the distant horizon until the last of the daylight faded into the black of night...and the moon rose, bright and golden and full of new promise...

'I'd like to come here every year,' Zac had said. 'Liv loved this place...and...and I reckon it helps.'

'Yes, it's important,' Chloe had agreed. Somehow, the sea and the wind, the wide open sky and the reassuring crash and thump of the surf seemed to help to soothe Zac's pain. 'We should definitely make it a tradition.'

Now, Zac turned and caught sight of Chloe at the bottom of the stairs.

'Hey,' he cried, his face lighting up. 'Lucy, look who's awake!'

'Mumma!' the baby girl shouted as she held out her chubby arms.

Still holding Lucy, Zac hurried over and slipped an arm around Chloe and kissed her. 'Merry Christmas, my bright-eyed girl.'

'Merry Christmas.' Chloe couldn't resist stroking his lovely bare chest. 'I hear you've been educating Lucy about Christmas traditions.'

'Like mistletoe?'

'Uh-huh.'

His eyes shimmered with secret amusement as he smiled at her. 'If you'd been listening carefully, you would know that there are one or two other traditions I'm reserving just for you.'

Chloe grinned. It was a promise she would definitely hold him to.

* * * * *

Mills & Boon® Hardback
November 2014

ROMANCE

A Virgin for His Prize	Lucy Monroe
The Valquez Seduction	Melanie Milburne
Protecting the Desert Princess	Carol Marinelli
One Night with Morelli	Kim Lawrence
To Defy a Sheikh	Maisey Yates
The Russian's Acquisition	Dani Collins
The True King of Dahaar	Tara Pammi
Rebel's Bargain	Annie West
The Million-Dollar Question	Kimberly Lang
Enemies with Benefits	Louisa George
Man vs. Socialite	Charlotte Phillips
Fired by Her Fling	Christy McKellen
The Twelve Dates of Christmas	Susan Meier
At the Chateau for Christmas	Rebecca Winters
A Very Special Holiday Gift	Barbara Hannay
A New Year Marriage Proposal	Kate Hardy
A Little Christmas Magic	Alison Roberts
Christmas with the Maverick Millionaire	Scarlet Wilson

MEDICAL

Playing the Playboy's Sweetheart	Carol Marinelli
Unwrapping Her Italian Doc	Carol Marinelli
A Doctor by Day...	Emily Forbes
Tamed by the Renegade	Emily Forbes

Mills & Boon® Large Print
November 2014

ROMANCE

Christakis's Rebellious Wife	Lynne Graham
At No Man's Command	Melanie Milburne
Carrying the Sheikh's Heir	Lynn Raye Harris
Bound by the Italian's Contract	Janette Kenny
Dante's Unexpected Legacy	Catherine George
A Deal with Demakis	Tara Pammi
The Ultimate Playboy	Maya Blake
Her Irresistible Protector	Michelle Douglas
The Maverick Millionaire	Alison Roberts
The Return of the Rebel	Jennifer Faye
The Tycoon and the Wedding Planner	Kandy Shepherd

HISTORICAL

A Lady of Notoriety	Diane Gaston
The Scarlet Gown	Sarah Mallory
Safe in the Earl's Arms	Liz Tyner
Betrayed, Betrothed and Bedded	Juliet Landon
Castle of the Wolf	Margaret Moore

MEDICAL

200 Harley Street: The Proud Italian	Alison Roberts
200 Harley Street: American Surgeon in London	Lynne Marshall
A Mother's Secret	Scarlet Wilson
Return of Dr Maguire	Judy Campbell
Saving His Little Miracle	Jennifer Taylor
Heatherdale's Shy Nurse	Abigail Gordon

Mills & Boon® Hardback
December 2014

ROMANCE

Taken Over by the Billionaire	Miranda Lee
Christmas in Da Conti's Bed	Sharon Kendrick
His for Revenge	Caitlin Crews
A Rule Worth Breaking	Maggie Cox
What The Greek Wants Most	Maya Blake
The Magnate's Manifesto	Jennifer Hayward
To Claim His Heir by Christmas	Victoria Parker
Heiress's Defiance	Lynn Raye Harris
Nine Month Countdown	Leah Ashton
Bridesmaid with Attitude	Christy McKellen
An Offer She Can't Refuse	Shoma Narayanan
Breaking the Boss's Rules	Nina Milne
Snowbound Surprise for the Billionaire	Michelle Douglas
Christmas Where They Belong	Marion Lennox
Meet Me Under the Mistletoe	Cara Colter
A Diamond in Her Stocking	Kandy Shepherd
Falling for Dr December	Susanne Hampton
Snowbound with the Surgeon	Annie Claydon

MEDICAL

Midwife's Christmas Proposal	Fiona McArthur
Midwife's Mistletoe Baby	Fiona McArthur
A Baby on Her Christmas List	Louisa George
A Family This Christmas	Sue MacKay

Mills & Boon® Large Print
December 2014

ROMANCE

Zarif's Convenient Queen	Lynne Graham
Uncovering Her Nine Month Secret	Jennie Lucas
His Forbidden Diamond	Susan Stephens
Undone by the Sultan's Touch	Caitlin Crews
The Argentinian's Demand	Cathy Williams
Taming the Notorious Sicilian	Michelle Smart
The Ultimate Seduction	Dani Collins
The Rebel and the Heiress	Michelle Douglas
Not Just a Convenient Marriage	Lucy Gordon
A Groom Worth Waiting For	Sophie Pembroke
Crown Prince, Pregnant Bride	Kate Hardy

HISTORICAL

Beguiled by Her Betrayer	Louise Allen
The Rake's Ruined Lady	Mary Brendan
The Viscount's Frozen Heart	Elizabeth Beacon
Mary and the Marquis	Janice Preston
Templar Knight, Forbidden Bride	Lynna Banning

MEDICAL

200 Harley Street: The Soldier Prince	Kate Hardy
200 Harley Street: The Enigmatic Surgeon	Annie Claydon
A Father for Her Baby	Sue MacKay
The Midwife's Son	Sue MacKay
Back in Her Husband's Arms	Susanne Hampton
Wedding at Sunday Creek	Leah Martyn